SIT DOWN TIME

GIL HARDWICK

Published by **eNovella Australia**, Perth, Western Australia

Typesetting, Layout and Cover Design by **Site211 Media**

This edition printed and bound by *https://www.createspace.com/*

National Library of Australia Cataloguing-in-Publication entry:

Author: Hardwick, Gil.

Title: Sit Down Time / Gil Hardwick.

ISBN: 978-0-9923704-5-9 (paperback)

Target Audience: For young adults.

Subjects: Coming of age fiction, Young adult fiction.

Dewey Number: A823.4

For Paul

Contents

PART THREE

Prologue

All he was trying to think about right at that moment was to keep his breathing steady, and get the notes out right. He nearly blew it. Just as the final high note of the Last Post left his cornet a family of magpies up in the treetops began to warble and he flashed an eye in their direction. But it came out OK.

During the long solemn moment of the minute's silence while the sky brightened and the sun rose they burst into full trill, stealing his thunder. The soldier standing next to him, noticing his distraction, gave him a quick nudge. He lifted the cornet again to his lips, and exactly on cue began playing Rouse, the short version not the full military wake-up call, but it was that sound of Reveille accompanied by the magpies up in the trees that pierced his soul nonetheless. In years to come that sound with its exquisite harmonies would return to haunt him, time and again; the only thing anywhere near like it the Pied Butcher Birds rousing the world in bright full song up north in the Kimberley.

They had offered him the same post at the full service later in the morning, after the march, but he declined pleading he was still a kid, and maybe a corporal from the military band should play the bugle, properly. The real reason was they were heading bush on Thursday and his mind was there, not here. His father had been offered the job of bringing the historic Ballard Hotel out on the top edge of the Nullarbor back into commercial viability, and decided to take it. The place was going broke and the company wanted to turn it around and put it back on the map.

Rouse done, the sun broke over the horizon and began to lighten the crowd gathered about in clusters under the trees. He bent down to begin packing up, but somebody called his name and he looked up to see a gaggle of journalists and people with cameras poking microphones at him, looking for catchphrases and headlines for tomorrow's paper - Alan Cameron Plays at Dawn Service - Boy Genius Honours the Fallen - ANZAC Triumph for Gifted Child Musician - all that stuff. He smiled and waved and held up his cornet, and had his Dad and Mum come stand next to him, then the corporal and some of the officers, and other sorts of dignitaries who were there but he didn't know.

They all disappeared abruptly leaving him with his parents standing there now in something of a daze.

The magpies had gone silent too, having claimed the day flown off somewhere in triumph. He bent down again and taking a soft cloth from his cornet case removed the mouthpiece and shook the spit out of the instrument and wiped it clean, then wrapping it placed it carefully back in its case and closed the lid, snapping the shiny brass catches shut as he did so.

PART ONE

Chapter One

The long day wore on, as flat and featureless as the broad horizon far ahead. From time to time, after a fuel stop or a relief stop for a pee along the way, he sat in the front car while his mother drove, then swapped around to ride with his Dad in the big truck following behind with their household stuff. He could reach the pedals in the station wagon all right, once Mum showed him how to move the front seat forward and let him drive for a while, but in the truck his legs were still too short, so Dad sat him in his lap so he could steer, and change gear while he worked the pedals.

He'd never really been very close to him, until now, except in their daily routine they usually shared the bathroom after he'd closed the bar and come in for a shower while he was in the bath, getting ready for bed, or got into the bath with him and they engaged in male small talk one on one. When he was little as his mother was busy with the day's till, it was he who contrived the routine so he could see his Dad at least sometimes, he knew. It isn't much fun for a boy to grow up alone in a big hotel, even a respectable establishment like theirs.

While Mum had her routine, apart from his long hours his Dad had a reserve about him, a quietness about him; the war she'd said one day, off-hand. Always dapper for a big man, well presented in tailored clothes, he could box and play footie as well, or so the men said.

The men in the bar always greeted him with respect and he ran a good pub, so he was happy with him and didn't question him. Stan Cameron was his own man, a man's man, and he was his son. He wanted to be just like him when he grew up, that's all he thought about him; as a son does, all and everything. Anyway he was busy himself with school, and getting homework done and his chores around the pub, and practicing his cornet and trumpet.

In his family they all worked hard, making a good go of it as they say.

Sitting in his lap in the truck across the wide flat plains, he could feel every part of him, the strength in his body, the sharp wit, clear muscle tone and ready reflexes; one with himself, and his steady hand on his own on the steering wheel. He knew he loved him and would do anything for him, without ever having to say it. But when he turned occasionally to catch his gaze there was something else. When he asked him once what it was like in the war, he merely shrugged and after a long drawn moment changed the subject, pointing out to him a flock of emus among the mulga and spinifex, or a mob of kangaroos, or a red wedge-tailed eagle working the insipid mid-Autumn thermals high above.

What they decided to do once they left the sandy mulga country and started across the great white salt pans further east, instead of driving through to arrive in Ballard in the wee small hours, was stop off at the Wallarabing Roadhouse for the night and start off again early next morning, and get there just after lunch. There was a motel next door which turned out to be clean and well-kept by a friendly middle-aged couple with children at university in Perth, the eldest already an anthropologist working for one of the communities further out while their son-in-law pumped fuel and ran the roadhouse.

Introductions out of the way, once they realised who their guests were the lady took Mum aside and together they did the kitchen while the men retired to the near-empty bar. Don, his name was, made Alan a real lemon squash in a midi glass while he and Stan each knocked back a pint of Guinness, on the house.

5

Chapter Two

Ballard turned out to be a pretty little place, nestled there beneath a looming breakaway just south of the Jack's Find mine, both named after old Jack Ballard, a bloke prospecting the area for gold way back in the 1860s who discovered the rich vein and brought a rush to the district. Some soul had long ago planted even rows of elegant Salmon Gums along the wide common with the same dusty bitumen strip passing for a main road going right through the middle, in the midst of which a ragged flock of rank goats rested from the noonday sun.

The grand old sandstone hotel trimmed with red brick stood out beyond the treed common like an American Southern mansion, but in the Federation style with its wide bullnose verandas; essentially modern and without the high neo-classic portico and fluted columns with their old-world pretence, though it asserted itself with the same singularly majestic presence. At one end of the front veranda to the left was a large sign over the public bar, and at the other two smaller signs to advertise the local Ballard Post Office and Commonwealth Bank agency; joint tenants occupying the one small front room with its counter and ancient iron grill, post office boxes and huge safe still there from the old gold rush days.

Mum turned off the road and drove straight up to it, parking the station wagon in the shade on the southern end of the broad front veranda. Dad coming behind in the truck turned off to follow her but drove through instead to the sprawling red brick station homestead of a house among the trees behind the hotel proper. With the engine off amidst the sudden outback silence, winding down the window to listen, all Alan could hear was loud clatter of a gen-set further away under the scarp, and a pump whirring somewhere, and crows off somewhere else again loudly cawing their arrival.

As he jumped down from the truck a weathered old lady wearing a sun shade, spectacles and sleeves emerged from the post office to greet them, while some of the goats came trotting over to bleat and nibble at him, and a friendly pup appeared suddenly wagging its tail in greeting.

He badly needed to pee, but wanting to go inside to use the toilet he found the door locked. Instead he went along to the end of the front veranda and ducking around the side of the house relieved himself there, the dog following him still wagging its tail. He glanced down at it, some sort of dingo-red heeler cross by the look of it, not much more than a pup; gangly, all paws and legs, but with bright eyes and pointy ears, and a bright wet tongue. He smiled and it wagged its tail again, then finishing he shook himself and tucking himself in zipped his pants up, turned and stepped back up onto the veranda. The pup sniffed at the wet patch, and cocking its leg added a quick yellow squirt of its own before bounding happily after its new best friend.

At the back the veranda also extended right across, except along the Post Office end was a long enclosed sleepout, in the old days used to accommodate out-of-pocket prospectors, and the drunks sleeping off their hangover. Out from the sleepout was a meat house enclosed in mesh and fly wire, with two goat carcases hanging in it. Next to that was a big chiller unit that looked as if it might be mounted on the back of a truck, mounted now on a steel platform with a couple of steps up into it. Beyond that again was a large double demountable house also on steel stumps, which looked fairly new. At the other end of the veranda near the kitchen was a freezer from the motor of which came a steady hum and the blast of cooling fans. In between were the back doors of the kitchen, and of the hotel itself giving access he was to find out later to a long dark passage leading right through to the front bar.

A slight brown girl was striding purposefully across from the kitchen door. As she drew near she called loudly, "*Monsieur Cameron, n'est pas? C'est vous est-il pas? Où avez-vous été? De quoi s'agit-il? Nous vous attendons. Le monde entier est dans l'attente de vous.*"

His father turned to him, shrugging his shoulders helplessly.

The girl turned to him. "*Parle-tu français?*" she wanted to know.

"*Un petit peu, de l'école.* Ah, *seulement . . .* um . . . *la français d'un garçon d'école.*"

"*Bon. Que va faire. Et c'est votre père, Monsieur Cameron?*"

"*Oui. Mon nom est Alan. Qui êtes vous?*"

"*Je suis Monique. Je suis la chef, du cours.*"

He turned to his Dad standing there.

"Ah, this is Monique. She is the chef. She says everybody has been waiting for you."

At that point Mum emerged from the back of the hotel and waved them over. She had an Aboriginal woman by the arm, and Monique turned on her.

"*Dire cette stupide garçon je suis en attente n'est plus. Le monde entier est sérieusement emmerdait, avec les tous.* Yes, pissing me off, all of you. *Lui dire Darren est dans le pontage, avec les touches.*"

The woman shrugged as helplessly, then looking at Stan asked, "You the new boss, eh? You mob s'posed to be 'ere yesterday. Old boss buggered off. Said 'e wasn't waitin' no longer. Trouble on the road, did ya? Broke down, unna?"

"No." Alan stepped forward. "We didn't break down. We stopped for the night at Wallarabing. Nobody said there was a hurry to get here. What's going on? Who are you, anyway?"

"V'ronica, boss," she stared daggers at Monique. "Been work-im pub kitchen, long time. Too bloody long. That copper cunt been

8

lock 'im up Bunna. Wait for new boss, eh. You mob go get Bunna, she'll be right."

"Who's Bunna?"

"Yeah, that Darren. Properly name Darren 'Ayes, that's 'im. Puckim cripple, proper useless bastard. Go get 'im, eh, open up pub, open up 'ouse, she'll be right."

"Why is he in the lockup? What did he do?"

"Ah, nothin'. Copper just bein' a cunt. Wants you mob go get him, fuck you 'round; make you go up there first, eh?"

By then something of a crowd had gathered, scattering the goats. The pup sat loyally at heel while the stray goats clattered across the bare ground back under the dry dusty shade of the tall trees, and Alan looked up at his Dad in askance. He was staring knowingly into the far distance, then sighed and shrugged, and nodded to himself.

"What's locked?" he wanted to know. "What are you being locked out of?"

"*Où en êtes-vous . . . verrouillé?*" Alan translated.

They all looked at one another, then Monique said quietly, "Ze bar, le cellar, ze *cuisine*, ze freezer, *et la maison, cela.* Can only use bathroom and toilet, *et les salles privies.* For eating, must drive to roadhouse for takeaway. *Pas de vin, pas de bière, rien.*"

"Yeah, that's right. Can't get nothin'," the other lady repeated. "No tucker, no bloody grog, can't get in, eh."

Stan turned, and stepping over to the truck bent to open the toolbox behind the fuel tank, and opening it took out a jemmy bar. Then he stepped up into the cab and opening a suitcase took out a clean towel. He then took Alan by the shoulder and together they went up the veranda steps to the front door of the house. Stepping sideways to a front window, with the jemmy he broke the two bottom quarter panes, and carefully knocking out the short wooden joining frame and sharp glass splinters laid the towel across the sill.

"Bullshit, son," he murmured as he worked. "There'll be spare keys in the house. In the front room somewhere, front desk, bottom drawer at the back. Maybe second bottom draw, have a look. Insurance will fix the window, or we'll do it ourselves. Get the spare keys for me, eh?"

"Don't tell anyone. When you find them, come out of the front door like normal and go across and open up the pub. Don't look at me. Hold your head up and say nothing. Don't say anything to anyone, not even your mother. Take control, be the boss. Set the example, son, we'll be right."

"What about the police?"

"They can get stuffed."

That was the very first time in his life Alan heard his father utter a profanity. It was the last thing he expected of him. Reddening, he was glad they were alone together with their backs to the crowd, and nobody could hear them. Only, as he climbed through the broken window pane the half dingo pup at his feet was still wagging its tail, wet pink tongue lolling out the side of its jaw, eyes bright and ears pricked in anticipation.

Later when the front bar was closed and the house shut down for the night, as he was taking his bath his father came in and said he was not to shower or bathe with him any more; he was a big boy now, and their world had shifted on its axis. Things could no longer be the same between them; this was serious and they'd have to watch out for themselves.

Chapter Three

The new day began bright and clear, though the sounds and smells were different and the air was bone dry, not like the coast at all. There were no early magpies that he could hear, but galahs and corellas, maybe a few cockatoos, and the goats.

There were voices coming from the hotel, so he dressed and went into the bathroom to wash his face and comb his hair, then went out through the front door to walk across. The red pup was there on the doorstep, getting up as he emerged to come over wagging its tail, tongue lolling and ears pricked up looking for adventure. It had a lot of fleas still, and probably a few other things, and while she fed it from the kitchen herself Mum would not allow it inside the house.

He bent slightly to pat its head and scratch its ears, and it fell in behind him without missing a step, staying close at heel all the way across. He was impressed, and smiled down at it. At the back door of the pub it simply plopped against the wall, tail thumping the red brick paving and gazing bright-eyed up at him with a keen sharp look that said I'll be here when you come out.

There were two women in the kitchen, busying themselves with getting the big hotel started for the day, cooking early breakfasts for their one or two house guests along with the few strays hanging around the place. As he entered they turned as one to look at him.

"What's your name?" one of them wanted to know.

"Alan. And you're Veronica, is that right?"

She smiled, and turning to the other said, "This one Alice, sister b'long me, properly. Same mother, same father."

He glanced from one to the other, smiling back. "You both look alike. I thought you might be sisters. Do you have any kids? Are there other children here, other boys?"

11

"One boy, name Eddie, one little girl, call her Gracie. Their daddy Chinaman, eh. 'E Sam, that fella, that 'usband b'long me. Alice got no plurry kids, plurry 'usband no good, got no pecker that one. Lazy black bastard, that Andy, want jiggy-jig all day, good for nothing, work laundryman, that fella. Watch out Andy, don't let 'im on the grog. See 'im with grog, take it off 'im, all right."

They both giggled at that, then turned as one again to look at him.

"You nice boy, eh. Clever fella you, talk 'im Frenchie lingo. Talk that Monique properly, no worry, she 'appy now that girl. You good boy, love your daddy, love your mummy, that right?"

"Yes, of course," he answered. Then he stood there shyly for a long moment, embarrassed by their frankness, not knowing what to say.

"What you like breakfass, Alan? Chop, sausage, bacon 'n egg? Scramble egg? We make toast; marmalade, apricot jam, plum jam, eh, cuppa tea? You like 'im porritch? We make you porritch, all right. Get you sugar-bag 'oney, longa bush. You like sugar-bag? That Eddie, 'e good boy too, clever fella, get 'im sugar-bag, find 'im bush bee, little one, call 'im sugar-bag fly, that one, get 'im bush 'oney, properly. You sit down 'ere, eh, we make 'im porritch you, tomorrow get 'im sugar bag. Good boy, no worry, we look 'im after you orright. Properly."

"Ah, yeah, that sounds good. Porridge, and scrambled eggs, and a cup of tea please. Yes. Do you have any fruit, or fruit juice?"

Alice began working at the stove while Veronica stepped out onto the veranda and called out.

Presently a couple of kids came running in, a boy his age about the same height, and a girl a year or two younger; 9 or 10 perhaps, both stopping suddenly just inside the door to stare wide-eyed the moment they saw Alan sitting there at the table. They were plainly part-Asian, both of them lithe and slim, tan with wavy black hair and very good looking, and he smiled at them.

They continued standing there until Alice had their porridge ready and set places for them at the table, and they sat cautiously, still staring at Alan. The mood was broken when Mum came in to see the three children sitting there.

"Well, what have we here?" she said, looking across at Veronica.

"That's my kids," she said, smiling. "That one Eddie, 'nother one Gracie. B'long Sam Cheong, Chinee gardener b'long Ballard, b'long this place. That one 'usband b'long me."

Elsie glanced from one to the other. "Do we have any more? Are there more of them? We'll have enough to start a school. Do they go to school?"

"'Ome school, missus. Other missus been teach 'em, properly. She buggered off now, not 'ere any more. Can't find 'nother one, not yet."

"Three more kid b'long that copper bastard," she went on quietly, "'is missus piss off, went back Perth. Took 'im kid with 'er. No good, city people, useless bastard, eh. 'Nother two b'long Andy sister, nephew b'long we, up railway camp, Walilya Siding. Big mob kid there now. Too many. School there, teacher out there, doctor, 'ospital, properly, eh."

"Is that right? What are they doing there? My mother is school principal at Lake Marnma, we were wondering where they all came from."

"Boss copper don't want 'em 'ere, missus. Clear ev'rybody out. All that mob b'long railway camp now, properly mission mob. Men working ranger, Victoria Springs, 'nother mob sit down b'long 'Ome Lake Station, further out."

"We'll see about that!" His mother stood only a moment frowning deeply, and then turned suddenly and stormed out, leaving Veronica frowning after her.

She turned to Alan, head cocked, curiously watching him. After a long moment, glancing at the door and back again, she asked him, "What name that mother b'long you, properly, Alan?"

"Elsie. Her name is Elsie."

"No, what name family. What mob she b'long, that one?"

"Ah, Forrestal. Her father is Jim Forrestal. Her mother is Dulcie Arthur. She is a Forrestal. She grew up on Home Lake Station, the same place. Her father is a teacher at Lake Marnma, as well. Her uncle, my great uncle Harry, he's the manager on Home Lake now, but the family still own the place."

"Jim Forrestal mob, that mob? Poppie Jim mob? 'Ome Lake mob, properly?"

"Yes. Old Jim, Poppie Jim, he's my great grandfather."

Chapter Four

"What yer doin' there, son? What ye think yer doin'?"

Alan turned to see where the voice was coming from. There was an old bloke at the end of the back veranda leaning against the post, watching him. As he looked again, it seemed he wasn't so old but bent and broken, as if he had been in some bad sort of accident.

"Um, just chopping a bit of firewood. I thought I'd do some kindling for tomorrow."

"That's not your job. Let the boys do it. Don't take their work away from them, eh?"

He stood holding the axe, eyeing him curiously. The pup got up from lounging at his feet and went over to the veranda, tail wagging though not so vigorously, more respectfully. He watched it for a long moment before glancing up again, squinting against the sunlight.

"You Bunna, are you? You the butcher? Cops let you out of jail, did they?"

"Ah, none o' your cheek, boy. It's Mr Hayes to you."

"Mr Hayes. Sorry. I'm Alan."

"Alan. Nice looking boy. Where ye get yer looks from? Yer Dad's not that handsome. How old are ye?"

"Ah, Mum I think. Her brothers are pretty good looking too, and so is she. But yeah, I'm 11, nearly 12. I'm starting Year 7, except I have to do it by School of the Air now."

Bunna stood looking at him without saying anything, but he held his gaze.

"What happened to you?" he asked finally. "You look like a tank drove over you. In a war or something, were you?"

"What, yeah, ah, separate. Wasn't Vietnam; that was different. Flamin' truck rolled on me, eh. In a coma 10 months. Titanium rods up me back. Bit of frontal lobe damage, where I cracked me scone; forget things, ye know. Good thing maybe, I reckon."

A voice called out from the kitchen and Bunna turned and called back he'd be there in a tick, giving the moment back to Alan, breaking his train of thought.

"Who's supposed to be doing the kindling, and chopping the firewood? Whose job is it?" Alan wanted to know, glancing back down at the chopping block. "Tell him if he doesn't do it properly I'll do it, and he won't have a job. Is that right?"

"Could be. Go and tell Alice, eh? Tell 'er if that Andy of 'ers in the laundry doesn't get up off his lazy black arse he's got the sack. That'll shift 'im."

"I will."

The same voice came loudly from the kitchen, "Bloody 'eard that, puckim white bastard, useless prick. White cunt you are. Give you puckim what-for! Next time that copper bastard picks you up, bloody leave you there, eh. You can rot there, unna."

Bunna only winked and surprisingly quickly for a cripple vanished somewhere.

He didn't worry about the barrow, but bending over picked up a good armful of split mulga and crossed the broad veranda with it, stacking it neatly outside the back door before coming back for another load.

Inside Mum and Monique were head to head over something, Mum quietly in control and keeping things on an even keel as they progressed through the pantry and freezer taking stock, jotting things down on her list.

Dad was calling him from the front bar so he made his way down the cool dark passage and poked his head through the door.

"How would you like a run back across to Kal in the truck, son? It needs to be back at the depot by Monday, that's tomorrow. Bunna can drive. Mr Keenan is bringing some stores up from Wallarabing for us in his van, and he'll give you a lift back, OK?"

"Yeah, OK, except Bunna can't drive. They won't let him have a licence. You'll have to get Andy or Sam to drive. Get Sam, I think, and Eddie can come too."

"Who is Sam?"

"Ah, he's the gardener, the Chinese guy. He's married to Veronica, Andy and Alice's brother-in-law. That's their son, Eddie, that boy, you know. It's his old house and pump shed way down the back, under the big overhang off the breakaway where it's always shady. There's water there too, a huge perched water table on top of the old rock bed running out from under the scarp, lot's of it."

His father was watching him intently. "All right, show me later. When you get back from Kal we'll go and have a good look around. Right now I need to get the truck back. Go ask him if he'd like to drive it back for me, there's a good lad."

"And Dad?"

"Yes, what?"

"Can I keep the pup? Take him with us? His name's Eric. I'll take him to the vet and have him vaccinated, and buy him a collar, and get him registered, OK?"

"Sure you can, Alan. Eric, is it? You look after him. It's good for a boy to have a dog, sorry you weren't allowed to have one at The Federal. That was one of the reasons we came out here, for your sake. We'll make it up to you, all right?"

"Great, thanks Dad."

He ran back down the passage and out the back door, flying past the kitchen and out across the common, the new pup loping along after him, and through the trees past their house down to the old pump shed.

Half an hour later they were in the truck at the roadhouse, Sam filling the tank with distillate.

The pup had its front paws up on the window sill, hanging its head out, tongue lolling. Alan turned to pat it and noticed somebody watching them through the front window, talking on the phone to somebody.

He turned to Eddy. "Who's that?" he wanted to know.

The other barely glanced his way, but called softly to Sam to hurry up.

It was too late. By the time he finished filling the tank and was coming back to the truck after paying the bill, a white and blue patrol car was pulling up behind them. Two burly police in uniform got out and approached him.

"Goin' somewhere, are you, Sam?"

"Just take 'im truck Kalgoorlie, then come back. Come back tomollo. OK, bye bye."

"Ah, not so fast, eh? Who you got with ya?"

"Two boys. Take two boys for lide, come back tomollo, OK."

One of them sauntered over to the truck.

"Who are you?"

"Alan Cameron, sir."

"That your dog?"

"Yes, sir. I'm taking it to Kal, to register it. I'm taking it to the vet too, for a check-up."

The policeman eyed him for a long moment.

"Need a permit to keep a dingo, know that, son?"

"No, I do not. That's not true. In South Australia you can't keep dingoes, but in Queensland and the Northern Territory to keep them you need a permit. Here they only have to be registered like an ordinary dog. Anyway it's not a dingo it's a Red Heeler. All I need to do is register it with the shire, and put a collar and tag on it, and I can keep it. I rang them and found out, they told me. That's where we're going, and taking the truck back. It has to be in the depot tomorrow."

"Smart-arse, are ya? Want to argue with me, do ya?"

"What? No, you asked me, and I'm telling you the truth."

The policeman turned away, cocking his head to his partner still standing there on the tarmac with Sam, while Eddie staring straight ahead through the windscreen gave Alan a sharp nudge with his elbow trying to shut him up. He was rigid, face ashen and lower lip trembling slightly, his knees shaking, but Alan merely frowned, confused.

"Looks like one of the litter that escaped from the pound the other day," the other policeman was saying, "or someone let them out. What would you know about that, Eddie, you fuckin' little shit?"

"Don't know nothin', boss. Know nothin' 'bout it, nobody let dogs out, I swear."

But the other wasn't listening anyway. He was eyeing Alan.

"Cameron boy, are ya? From the pub?"

"Yes, sir. Alan."

"Break and enter there, Friday morning. What would you know about that?"

"What? No, there wasn't. That's not true. All we had to do was get the spare keys from the house, so we could open the hotel. Somebody had the place locked up. I don't know."

"Why didn't you just come over and get them?"

"Get them from where? Where would I get them? Somebody called Bunna had them, and you had him in the lockup, somebody said . . . Veronica said . . . that's all. They could have been left at the Post Office, if it's that important. What's going on? Nothing to do with us."

The two cops glanced at one another, then the second said to him, "I think you'd better come to the station with us, son. Answer a few questions."

Alan shrugged, and sighed, then unseen by the police Eddie nudged him again so he stepped down from the truck. Turning unthinking to whistle for the pup to follow, suddenly amid loud yelling the engine started and the truck drew quickly away, Eddie holding the pup by the scruff and reaching over as they veered out onto the road to slam the door shut.

The second cop spun on his heel to catch Sam but it was too late, he had already disappeared around the back of the truck to the driver's side, and mounting the cab as Alan stepped down onto the driveway shouted at Eddie to "glab the dok! Hully! Shut puckin' door quick! Bugger off real quick, bastard going shoot dok, no-good stupid puckin' *gwai-lo*! Get going right now! Alan, see you, no wolly, we legister dok, take 'im vet. Get your father come, bye bye, we going now, you'll be right."

By the time anyone could react the truck was already out on the main road and away, engine revving and churning up the gravel; Sam still yelling shrilly at the top of his voice but in sheer panic by this time indecipherably in rapid-fire Cantonese. A great shrieking flock of galahs took off from the adjoining paddock, adding to the cacophony as they wheeled away above the tree tops, then as quickly everything went quiet again while Sam managed to change gear finally to be riven and disembowelled, swallowed and digested by wavering heat shimmer on the distant horizon.

Half an hour later Alan's mother, not his father, arrived at the police station to retrieve her son. Back outside in the station wagon she sat stone-faced jotting names and serial numbers in her little notebook, then tucked it into her handbag before reaching over to take Alan by the hand, wanting to know if he was all right.

Chapter Five

Monique was upset about having to shift out of her room in the hotel into the house, but Mum was taking no nonsense from her. They were going to be busy all day with the whole place to be cleaned from top to bottom, stores arriving this evening and two full busloads of prepaid guests arriving around mid-day tomorrow.

Since Alan had missed his ride to Kalgoorlie and had no jobs scheduled, she called him to help. With big brother Eddie away with her father and no pup for the moment to follow him devotedly around, Gracie had attached herself to him. When Mum called they both appeared.

When he found out what was being asked of him, Alan went off to rummage through his belongings and find his school French dictionary, but by the time he returned Gracie was already talking to her in passable English. Mum had by then walked away from the argument, washed her hands of it, except the moment Alan returned with his dictionary Monique lapsed back into formal French and was waving her arms about.

Alan stood consulting his dictionary, letting her vent her frustrations, until finally he took a deep breath and spoke to her as if reading a speech.

"It is better if you live with us in the house, Monique, and be part of the family. It's no good for you to live by yourself in the hotel, and besides we need the extra room. We want you to help us with our school work. Mum is too busy running the house. Even Dad has extra work to do, he will have to do the till and the banking now, as well as the bar."

She stared at him. "*De quoi parlez-vous, garçon? Je ne suis pas un au pair! Je suis le chef!*"

"*Oui,*" he replied patiently, thumbing through the dictionary, "*c'est important. Vous êtes la chef d'cuisine employées ici, pas*

22

d'hotel. But this is Australia, *nous avons besoin de travailler ensemble.* We don't have anyone else. Anyway I'm not going to stand here trying to translate for you every time you throw a wobbly."

"In the morning Veronica and Alice will prepare all the breakfasts for everyone, while you sleep in after working late." he went on slowly, deliberately, "During the day, while they clean the rooms you can help with the children. Then they will help mother with a light lunch. In the afternoon and evening while Dad runs the bar you are the chef, responsible for serving dinner."

"And you are not from Metropolitan France, you are from Madagascar, Monique, here on a work permit. You don't have to pretend, it's all right. *Ce n'est pas un problème pour vous.* OK? How much extra do you want?"

"That's it? That's all you have to say?" she replied. "Well, all right, $150.00."

He thought a moment, running through the figures. "That's fair enough, yes, OK. $150.00 extra. Good. Gradually we can take you up from the kitchen, and the main bar, and for your next job you can say you were our *chef de maison*, with a big responsibility. OK?"

She simply nodded slightly, staring more intently at him, until he called out, "*Ma mère, C'est que tous les droit?*"

"*Oui,*" she called back. "Bravo. *Bien fait. Mais dire que fille, si elle veut que le travail qu'elle peut parler Anglais, et montrer du respect. Je sais qu'elle est un enseignant d'ecole. J'ai lu son reprendre. Dites-lui qu'elle ne vit pas avec les ignorants sauvages*, do you hear me, Monique?"

Monique stood back, eyes wide.

"Who are you people?"

"Ah, well," Alan said quietly, almost to himself, "ah, Mum's a bit funny you know, a bit of a larrikin. She grew up on a cattle station. When she was a little she was sent off to the new Perth Contemporary College, then off to some fancy finishing school, like, in Switzerland. She has an Honours degree in Microbiology and a second degree in Oenology and Viticulture, Certificate. IV in Microbusiness Operations and in Catering Management, and she has a graduate diploma in Tourism Development. And she's a licenced publican. That's why we're here."

"She's big on women's liberation too, so watch out she doesn't take any bullshit from anyone. But she's got this sense of humour as well, makes me laugh. When she was young she was going to be an actress, and she can hell play the piano. She accompanies me when I play the trumpet. If we can find a good bass player we can start a jazz ensemble. Outback jazz, way out in the desert, it's in the business plan, they showed me and we talked about it."

"Do you understand what we want to do here, Monique? It's going to be just great, but we all have to work together, like I said." His eyes shone with enthusiasm.

"Once we're settled in here we plan to have authentic bush tucker on the menu, using saltbush and native herbs, tanami apples, pepperberry, and finger limes and desert limes, and plums, and quandongs. There are other nuts too, like macadamias and bunya nuts, with mango, and when he gets back Eddie's going to tell me about sugar-bag honey, and we'll have kangaroo tail soup, and wallaby and emu, and Murray Cod and yabbies and rack of goat."

In the event, apart from her pride and joy; a set of beautiful hand-forged and very expensive Japanese chef's knives, she didn't have much in the way of belongings; only what she could fit in her backpack. Alan was impressed with her knives, which she plainly knew how to use, and after that showed her a great deal more respect. Once relocated to the house she smiled at him.

Gracie too turned out to have a keen sense of humour; robust, down to earth like her mother and auntie, but as he was to find out some of her father's rapid-fire delivery. She was a different matter entirely. Once Monique began to settle into her new room, rather than allowing Alan to go back to the hotel to help with the cleaning, she took his hand and led him around the back of the house and down toward Sam's orchard and vegetable gardens.

He glanced down at her. She was scratching the palm of his hand with her little finger, not looking at him, so he pulled his hand gently away. She just smiled and said nothing.

"Where are you taking me?" he wanted to know.

"Show you garden, orchard. That Sam, 'e good gardener, plenty fruit, vegetable. No worries."

But she had a look about her, the way her eyes flashed at him. Fore-armed, he nodded slightly and she led the way.

She was right. Sam's gardens were lush and productive. He plainly worked hard at it, with new mangoes and avocados growing alongside the old established oranges, figs and olives. He had rows of tomatoes, scallions, onions and garlic, lemon grass, bok choy and pak choy, lettuce and celery, with ginger sprouting from the warm damp soil beneath the rock face, and sprawling fields of melons.

Alan shook his head in amazement. She led the way through the orchard to a rough shady bush bower, partly converted to a greenhouse with old window frames and car windscreens, to show him rows of pots of macadamia and spiky bunya seedlings that would soon be ready to plant out, come late winter.

He didn't know what to say, just smiled, and she took his hand again and they went inside the ramshackle old house.

She showed him around, going from room to room. The place was clean and tidy. Plainly she wanted to impress him; to show him the family was good, respectable, not rubbitch. She watched him closely but he still didn't say anything. Eddie's room was scattered with normal boy's stuff; some books but mostly toys and games, while in her room the bed was made and her girl's things arranged neatly, but they bypassed her parent's room and led the way straight through to the big old kitchen.

There wasn't a lot there. The family had their meals mostly in the hotel kitchen so Gracie had made the place her own, and sitting her guest at the table busied herself making him lunch.

Toward late afternoon the day was still hot. By then the pair of them were at the waterhole for a swim, when Eric came bounding through the light scrub wearing his new collar and bright shiny registration tag. He stopped at the edge of the water, leaning forward to quickly lap with his pink tongue, but then stood there front paw up and tail wagging, staring at Alan to come out.

As he emerged from the water Eddie appeared, to stop suddenly. He glanced between Alan standing there naked, and his sister also plainly naked still partly in the water, his face set.

"What?" Alan wanted to know.

"What you doin' with that sister?"

"Eh? Nothing. What do you mean?"

Alan paused, cocking his head.

"Maybe you should ask her what she's doing with me, more like it."

Eddie glanced at her there in the water, but she only stared him down.

"What's the matter you? Nothing," she said "'E look same like you, just a boy. I didn't laugh, no worry you. What's up?"

Alan looked sharply around at her, and she grinned. By then the pup was jumping up wanting his attention. He smelled a bit of flea bath or something. Without saying anything he bent down to retrieve his t-shirt and dried himself, then pulled on his underpants and shorts. Gracie likewise emerged from the water and dried herself with her loose floral cotton dress, then slipped it over her head and tied the stitched belt around her waist. She wasn't wearing panties anyway, and her small budding girl's breasts pressed against the wet fabric; her long wet hair still dripping.

With a quick glance at Eddie they turned and disappeared down the track in the direction of the house.

Chapter Six

"Do you have anything to tell me, Alan?" Mum wanted to know.

"What? No. Nothing. What are you talking about?"

"The women are up in arms about you and Gracie. I only want to know if anything untoward happened between you."

"Ah, no, it wasn't anything. It was hot, and we went for a swim . . . just, like, skinny dipping that's all. Eddie came up and got the wrong idea. Anyway, Mum, you know me better than that, I'm not a little boy any more. You just have to trust me. Don't you trust me?"

She turned to look at him, nodding quietly to herself. "Yes, I trust you. That's not the problem. You simply don't know these people very well. Anything between you and Gracie makes things complicated, that's all."

"How? What's complicated about me having a girlfriend? Aren't I old enough by now?"

She glanced up sharply. "Girlfriend? I thought you said there wasn't anything between you."

"What? What do you mean? Like, we didn't have sex or anything like that. I didn't even have, like, you know, a stiffy. Anyway the water was cold. She's nice, that's all, she's fun to be with. She didn't do anything with me. We were just swimming and having fun. That's all I mean."

She frowned, looking quizzically at him with a slight shake of her head, then paused.

"There is a huge difference between a sister and a girlfriend, Alan," she said finally. "Among these people it is two different planets."

"But she's not my sister. We didn't do anything. What are you talking about?"

"OK. Well, no, maybe it's not your fault, but the girl has fallen in love with you. She broke the rules, and it can make things difficult for us. Let me explain. Tribally, those two ladies and I are sisters. That dates all the way back to your great-grandfather Jim Forrestal's time. I have to say I'd forgotten about it, you know. Somebody must have raised it, or said something."

She was looking at him again.

"Anyway, you are no longer little but you are still a boy," she went on. "There are certain things you don't know yet. Veronica and Alice were thinking all you kid mob will be brothers and sisters, then we can be mother mob to you all and the hotel can be run as one big happy family. In their culture, everybody has to be adopted into some sort of kinship arrangement otherwise they are unable to relate properly, or use the proper form of address. But if you and Gracie are betrothed, that makes them your in-laws, all of them, and they must avoid you."

"What? We're not betrothed! You mean, engaged to be married? No, we're not! That's not right, what a silly idea."

"Well, no, not formally, but if you go down that road it qualifies you to marry; same thing. It's not silly. She is in love, it's the most serious thing among them. Alan, you simply can't. Gracie is your sister. What she is doing is called "wrong way". She is being punished for it and will have to stay home for the next week or so until it sorts itself out, when I wanted to get school started. Traditionally you would be punished too, taken bush and speared in the leg or worse, being the boy. You mustn't interfere. You must promise me, Alan, not to do anything, or say anything."

He stood stunned, but she went on.

"All right, son, for the next week while Gracie is grounded, you will help your father in the bar, and with whatever jobs he has for you. When you are in the kitchen for your meals you will keep your face down and eyes averted, and show respect. You will not speak to anybody unless you're spoken to. Is that clear? I'll let you know when things are back to normal."

He stood his ground for the moment, still thinking.

"What happens if we fall in love? Did you think about that? Did any of you think about that, or ask me first?"

She nodded wisely, patiently.

"If that's the way you truly feel, Alan, you must say absolutely nothing, not to anybody. If you still feel the same way when you are grown you must both go away somewhere, live somewhere else. You cannot come back here. That's a serious decision you must think very carefully about, because if you do that, to these people you will both be dead. You are a nice boy and they will cry for you, but you can never return to this part of the country. Think about what you will be giving up. Your family is here; these are our lands too, we have all agreed."

"Go on now, off you go. Go ask your Dad if he has any jobs he wants done. There is the cellar that needs to be tidied and restocked, and we still have to go over our prices. Keep yourself busy, Alan, and keep your head down for the next week. It's a test for you, I know, and people will be watching how you handle it."

He watched her face for a long moment, then turned and left. He went down the passage to the bar to find his father, but he wasn't there. He found him out the front sweeping the veranda.

"Dad," he called softly, upset.

"Hey, son. You OK? Not too rough on you, were they?"

"You know, do you?"

"Yep."

"What do you reckon?"

"Ah, well, always two sides to every story. I'm not too fussed about it."

"Will they hurt her, do you think?"

"Nah, don't think so. She'll be right. Just don't say anything, is that OK? We need to keep the house running smoothly. Just, sometimes it's a good idea not to open up too much to people you don't know very well, don't you think? Our family business is our family business."

"But is it true that I can never marry Gracie?" He stood his ground.

"Ah, don't take it so seriously. That sort of thing is far more important to your mother, it's not something I know much about. They're her people. What do you want to get married for?"

"Well, I don't, but, I mean, in principle . . . hypothetically, what if?"

"Your Mum is probably right, son, though it's not as if you're going to break up the tribe by it. Things are buggered up anyway, as bad as it gets, but you still have to give people a chance, and respect their culture."

"That's not what I meant."

"Yes, I know what you meant, Alan, but I'm not about to make your life decisions for you. I trust you, you're a bright boy, with a good heart and want to do the right thing. I can see that. But you can see yourself that it's an issue, so if you want to go down that path you're going to have to think very carefully about it. Just be discrete, all right, keep your mouth shut and learn to keep your feelings to yourself."

"You probably don't trust Eddie much right now," he went on thoughtfully, "but you'll have to sort that out with him as you go along. Maybe give Gracie some sign so she'll know how you feel, then both of you behave and do the right thing in the meantime."

"Do you really think so?"

"Um, son, what did you mother ask you to do? She wants me to give you something to do, is that right? Go and tidy the bottleshop for me, you know how to do it. There are five full pallets to unpack, then take the invoices and work out our buy-in cost for me. When you do the prices keep our cost-of-sale around 30%, don't be too rough on the customers, OK. We want people to know we're fair and reasonable, and run a good pub."

"Then, when you finish that, do the banking for me will you? Our daily takings are in the small safe in the house. I take them to the house after I close up of a night, but they need to be deposited at the bank every morning. If we get robbed we have no insurance cover. If the bank gets robbed it's on them at least. Old Mrs Robinson knows what to do. She'll show you."

After a few mornings helping Dad in the bar, then, Alan determined to stay away from the kitchen and leave women's business to the women. He was furious, the insult palpable. He found himself especially disappointed in his mother for not trusting him, as if she didn't really know him at all, paying no real attention to him all the time he was growing up, and he didn't like the way he was feeling about her. She was really very talented; highly intelligent and accomplished, but she didn't know the first thing about men or boys, he could see that now. It explained a lot of things.

All right, if they want mother-in-law avoidance, no problem. If they want stubborn, they'll get stubborn. No more trying to be nice. He knew now why men keep their feelings to themselves, to save having to put up with that sort of bullshit. They want properly clever fella, let's see what clever is.

He was up early and ate his porridge and scrambled eggs on toast every morning, and drained his cup of tea, but then promptly left the kitchen before anyone else arrived and went down to the bar to clean up and put things in order before Dad arrived to take over around 8:30. Once the bar opened and the odd bloke started coming in for an early drink, even though it was quiet he went back to the house to do some homework, and after an early lunch practiced on his trumpet.

As the early afternoon grew hot, he and Eric went down to the waterhole for a swim, skinny-dipping; he made a point of it. Being a desert dog he guessed, the pup simply refused to come into the water but sat on the bank waiting patiently for him, or lay belly down stretched out on the cool damp earth, or went running off a short distance sniffing around but always coming back to check he was still there.

By the third day it had become clear to everybody where his heart lay, but still he said nothing and neither did they. Then on the fourth day he could hear Gracie singing from the house, just at the time he went in for his swim, and finishing by the time he left.

At the start of the new week when Monique began supervising their schoolwork, just to make sure the message got through he moved his desk away from Eddie's, pushing it over against the far wall before placing Gracie's desk squarely between them. And that was that, so he thought.

Sam wasn't going to put up with any of it, however. After lunch one day as Alan was out on the back porch preparing for trumpet practice, he came over brandishing a bamboo flute to tell him he wasn't playing properly.

"What do you mean, I'm not playing properly? I'm a good player."

"No, not good enough," said Sam. "If you are average player, OK. But you are not average player, you are fine talent, but not good enough. If you are fine player, must be excellent."

"What?"

"Listen to me, I telling you. You are technically perfect, but have to make your instrument sing. No good pushing buttons, must sing. Must hear your breathing. OK? Now, start again. No trumpet, play cornet. Play sweet and warm, accompany flute, no jazz. Not yet. Start again, from beginning. I teach you."

Alan stood staring at him in amazement, but Sam wasn't putting up with that either. He put his flute to his lips, going up and down the scale, then stood back and said, "Come, come, Alan. Do it like that. Let me hear you, up and down."

He put down his trumpet and picked up the cornet and began to play, up and down the scale, feeling like a raw beginner. Sam listened intently, then played again on his flute, taking the lead. As he finished he pointed out to him, "You can hear difference, Alan. Come on, play again."

This time Sam accompanied him and he could hear the discord between the two. It was true, Sam's mastery of the humble bamboo flute was exquisite.

"Where did you learn to play like that," he asked, curious now, not realising they had attracted an audience.

Bunna, who'd been standing unnoticed at the end of the porch listening, stepped forward to interrupt him.

"That man is Dr Zhang Huá-wei, Alan," he said. "You should know. His name Cheong is lazy Hongkongese, but it's Zhang. He turns on the idiot ching-chong bullshit for the coppers, because they're such dead cunts that's all. He is a doctor and a soldier, and a scholar of Confucius. He was with me in Laos and Cambodia, special operations."

Alan turned his head in surprise. "Ha!" he replied. "I suppose you're going to tell me you're a famous psychiatrist or something."

They frowned, cocking their heads in unison at him.

"Well, anthropology, actually," Bunna said after a long steady pause. "Before the truck rolled on me, and did me head in. That was after we returned to Australia and I decided to go to uni. Then we came out here, to the desert, worked up at Walilya helping on Land Rights."

Sam interrupted him again, brusque and annoyed, shaking his head. "No, Alan, don't worry all that bullshit. Long time ago. Practice music, OK. Don't be second class, be number one. Look for better future, look after family; not look behind. No good."

Alan simply turned to face him, staring wide-eyed at him. Sam stared back, not unkindly, then putting his flute down on the chair turned back to him and took him firmly by the shoulders.

"You like my Gracie, Alan, I know," he said, quietly changing the subject. "You are good boy, behave yourself, but stubborn, *yìng qì*. Strong healthy boy, *mho jījī*; *hǎo shuài zi, qiáng jībā, guītóu, wei dàn*, no problem. My son tell me, you good strong body, good looking, make good strong baby, strong son. Can see young girl is beautiful, good heart, good brain, make good wife, but behave yourself, *mh'tsat, mh'puk gai*, just happy children swimming in water. You are good boy, good family. No live in gutter, no stupid. Family very happy."

"OK, you marry Gracie, but not yet. Too young. Must wait until young man, young woman, finish education first, learn to play music properly, get good job, make money, build house, then you can marry."

"What about Veronica? What about that wrong way business?"

"No, too far away. You are not so close, not like Walilya business, Home Lake business, not properly. Your mother cousin b'long my wife, not close-up sister. I am the father, don't worry so much. You father-in-law, my job keep everybody happy. Women only want family be happy, no fooling around. I fix for you, all right?"

He turned then and called out, and in a moment Eddie appeared with Gracie. It was obvious they had both been given a good talking to, and were waiting just out of sight. Sam took Eddie by the shoulder first and stood him in front of Alan.

"OK, no more bullshit. You shake hand. Be friend. Everybody happy."

When they'd done that Gracie stepped forward and kissed him lightly on the cheek, and said she was sorry for causing all the trouble but pressed her lithe body against his nonetheless, and held him close. She wouldn't be getting much chance for a long while so they let it go without saying anything.

The rule they all had to obey was that she not to swim with the boys, or show her body, or flirt with Alan. Shame. They too must be modest, and spend their time now with the men. They must work hard and show respect. They were no longer innocent, no longer considered children, not now. If they are betrothed they must conduct themselves properly in public, and Eddie mind his own business.

Chapter Seven

What Sam wanted Alan to do was start thinking in terms of concert standard when practicing his music, not just mucking around thinking he could play real jazz on nothing much more than his local brass band training. It was still a distraction in the house of an evening, and Mum needed a quiet place as a break from the hotel, so Sam made him come and practice in his study in the rambling old gardener's house down the back.

The walls were lined with books, thousands of them; most of them in Mandarin with yellow paper covers but many in English translation scattered among European classics. Gracie hadn't shown it to him, it was her father's private space, and anyway foreign to her mother's native way of thinking; entirely unexpected way out here in the middle of the desert.

There he played for him not only bamboo flute, but the piccolo and flute, recorder, oboe and clarinet. He discussed with him at length the relationships among the wind instruments, and the relationships between woodwind and brass in a full orchestra. This was new territory, so Alan listened intently. He was no longer surprised when Sam took out his Chinese two-string, *er-hu*, and played that instrument quite as delicately as he played piccolo and flute.

Ignoring her mother, Gracie got herself into the habit of making tea for them, and cooking them small biscuits and pastries and bringing them in for refreshment while they practiced. At times Alan could hear her singing in accompaniment while she worked, her lovely pre-formed voice still flute-like, not yet through the thin, reedy stage during full puberty in another year or two, yet with a huskiness already evident that made him stop playing at times to listen to her; holding his hand up to Sam to stop playing as well. Except when they stopped, after a moment she stopped too until they started again.

When he left Sam loaned him books to read, Lao-tsu's *Dao de-jing*, and Sun-tsu, *The Art of War*, and the Chinese classics; *Journey to the West*, *Romance of the Three Kingdoms*, and when he had a chance buried his nose in them. He withdrew and became quiet, watchful and alert, the pup constantly at heel unless he was actually inside the hotel when it sat patiently on the back veranda; not saying much to anybody; studiously doing his homework and hotel chores, working hard and practicing his music.

During the day Sam simply continued wearing his frayed peasant pyjamas and straw coolie hat as he potted about his garden, lovingly tending his seedlings, his fruit trees and his rows of vegetables, and likewise every day brought up big baskets of fresh produce for the kitchen and joined everyone in their joking banter, while with the house often full now with buses coming and going Bunna and Eddie did the butchering and supplied *capretto*, the house specialty, along with the more regular quarters of beef, sides of mutton, and whole lamb and pork he had trucked in from the west coast which he broke down himself depending on what Monique wanted.

Around the end of the second week of practice, Mum arrived unexpectedly and after a quick glance into the study went through to the old kitchen to speak to Gracie. He couldn't hear her sing after that, but next morning noticed Mum and Sam heads together in deep conversation. They both stopped to look at him as he stood watching them, but said nothing.

"*If that's the way they want to do things,*" he thought, wandering off still annoyed with them, "*not saying anything to me or telling me anything, bets are off.*"

He stopped what he was doing and went out the back, past the house and through the gardens, and went inside. Gracie was in the kitchen. As he came in she smiled, and came to him, holding him to her, but after a moment he held her slightly away.

"What's going on, Gracie? Tell me."

"Ah, no, it's all right. Your mother want to give me voice lesson, speaking lesson, singing lesson, make me lady. You too, singing lesson. Father talking 'er now, change around, practice music, practice voice, singing, you and me."

"Is that right? What about Eddie?"

"Ah, 'e no worry. Want to be stockman, slaughterman, ride 'im 'orse, that boy. Bring 'orse down from 'Ome Lake, your uncle coming too, maybe two-fella, two uncle mother side b'long you. Copper bastard no good, need more men 'ere keep 'im safe this place."

"Is that right? Why didn't they tell me? Why don't they tell me what's going on?"

"You been too much cranky bugger, Alan, no talk anybody. Work too 'ard. No good. Don' worry so much. Why you so cranky all a time? No good cranky, your beautiful eyes red and crazy, like you father. Make me frighten."

"What about Dad? What about him?"

"Too much trouble copper bastard. Don't you know?"

"No, I don't. I don't go near the bar after I finish of a morning. It's a bigger mess than it was, but now we're busy, of course. What else?"

She held her fingers to his mouth, murmuring to him to ask father, then she leaned forward to kiss his lips before pulling back suddenly, pushing him out of the kitchen.

"Go away now Alan. No good, we in trouble. I love you too much, want you too much. We too young. I wait for you, all right, only one for me. No other boy for me, all right. Now go."

But then she turned and walked back quickly through the kitchen and along the passage to her room, and closed the door. As he stood there he could hear her sobbing softly to herself.

He turned too then and went out the back door, bumping into Eddie on the way.

"Ah, looking for you," he said, a little too quickly. "Getting some horses. Want to teach me to ride?"

"Sure, no worry, we go sugar-bag, eh? You two uncle mob comin', 'Ome Lake side. Bring 'im 'orse. Two days, come Friday."

"Is that right? Where are we going to keep them?"

"Stable, over there, back there, 'nother side garden. From old time. We fix 'im up."

"Really? Do they need cleaning? Do you want a hand with it?"

"Yep, all right. We get Bunna, go fix 'im up stable, properly."

With new-found cause, he clucked his tongue and smacked his thigh lightly for the pup to come and the three of them went off to find Bunna. An hour later when Veronica came home from early kitchen duty in the hotel Gracie was still in her room, and she spent the rest of the afternoon gently brushing her long wavy black hair and talking quiet women's business to her too lovely, too intelligent and too much in love pubescent daughter still fuming at having been betrayed by her brother, and not trusted enough by her parents and family to be sensible.

Chapter Eight

"Alan, you do need to relax," Mum was saying, though he was annoyed with her still and not listening.

She had spent the past week with Gracie explaining to her the way the body changes during puberty, and how cartilage thickens and how that affects the larynx and singing voice. She was a natural athlete and singer with an easy rhythm and pulse and good breathing control. What she wanted to do with her over the next few years while her woman's body developed, aside from elocution and language acquisition, was keep her singing up and down the scale to prevent her voice splitting later into soprano or alto. And she was to do a lot more running and swimming, and holding her breath under water to build her lung capacity and muscle tone while she was still growing.

But Alan was resisting her, intransigent. He was angry with her, frustrated with her. She had always been dominant in the family while his Dad worked, and kept his own counsel, always on the excuse that he was a man, and a war veteran. He only knew him man-to-man because they had bathed together since he could remember; always after work, both male while she is female. She was liberated, but only with regard to women, and children he had to admit, but not men.

"Anger bottles up in the throat chakra, Alan," she was saying, "and affects the voice. It affects your breathing, tightens your bronchia and chest, like a dam about to break but never happening. Boy's voices change a lot more than girls, but the male voice with exercise and breathing can still be kept sweet, not course, gravelly . . . girls without proper voice training as they grow become screechy, stuck between soprano and alto, but men's voices are gravelly and angry. We need to fix that."

"I don't care, Mum. I don't want to do this, not with you. It's too technical, like. I'm real happy that you want to help Gracie, that way, but . . ."

He glanced away, thinking about the naturally easy knowing way Eddie was able to talk to his father about the body, and the tone of a man's body, and the way Sam knew about men's health, and being strong and healthy, and being a good man and a husband and father, and producing good strong children, and working hard and looking toward a better future, not backward all the time, when he and his Dad were to keep their body private; not to say or do a single thing in case they upset somebody, or offend somebody, and keep their thoughts privately to themselves . . . in case they are judged and found wanting . . . not in so many words but the same thing . . .

It wasn't fair. Why couldn't they talk about it the same way Mum was talking so easily about the throat and larynx, and being a good singer, and speaking well, and being a lady, like he could be learned and knowing and strong and a gentleman like Sam; like Dr Zhang Huá-wei given half a chance, and his Dad the way he wanted his Dad to be, the way he felt?

"What is it, son?"

He looked at her.

"Ah, nothing, Mum. It's OK, don't worry. I don't want to do it. Sorry, no I'm not sorry . . . I mean, now Uncle Dan and Uncle Harry are here with the horses, like, I want to learn to ride, properly. I'll keep practicing music with Sam, and reading, and doing my chores, I promise . . . and my schoolwork is good you can't complain about that, except Monique made me change the desks back around . . . he can help me with my voice, and my vocalising . . . no, bugger it . . . nothing else . . ."

His mind by then had gone wandering through the lush gardens, gone bush.

Nobody had ever spoken to him so critically, so clearly and eloquently as Sam; so connected with where he was right now in his life, with how he was feeling, exploring himself and looking at himself after his bath in the mirror and wondering about it, he and Gracie; putting the faults in his playing so precisely to him, while at the same time pointing him so well in another direction that he might want to think about.

That's what he wanted to know more about, and think about before he did anything else in his life. Like Dad said, it was his life decision to make.

Chapter Nine

There was nobody in the kitchen when he came in for breakfast. The place was a mess.

Alice hurried in after him, fussing about, avoiding his gaze, trying to think. Finally, almost apologetically she served him porridge and forgetting toast and eggs set about tidying the place.

Absently, automatically, she made up a pot of tea and filling his cup placed it before him, then went back without saying anything to scraping meal scraps into the bins and stacking dirty plates on the sink.

It hadn't been part of her job to make this boy his eggs on toast, and it didn't cross her mind. It was that drunken Andy bastard, that 'usband, somebody given 'im grog, make 'im crazy, no good bastard. Nobody say any'ting anybody. Properly buggered up, every'ting.

When Veronica came in soon after she saw Alan didn't have his eggs on toast so straightaway she started on them, making a fuss of it. While she was doing that he looked about, and shook his head and shrugged, and getting up went to the cold room and helped himself to orange juice, and some fresh apples they'd got in.

They still weren't speaking to one another - mother-in-law business - so he had no idea what was going on until Uncle Dan came in, closely followed by his twin Harry, and the women burst out into their usual loud bantering chatter. Taciturn men both of them, neither made any attempt to reply, faces set, and like Alan sat eating their breakfast and the place went quiet again.

Eventually, curiosity piqued, he asked what was up, to which Harry simply flicked his head back in the direction of the bar. He glanced over at Alice, then at Veronica and back at his two uncles to no avail, so putting down his knife and fork stood and went out, down the passage to the bar.

"Shit, eh?"

There was broken glass everywhere, the big front window stove in with Andy Yatjimarra's battered old Toyota ute nudged up against the front counter.

He turned to go back to the kitchen, but bumped into his Dad who must have come up behind him, bleary-eyed and cranky through loss of sleep when he should have been still in bed.

They didn't have much chance to exchange news before the white and blue patrol car pulled up out front, so early, the sun barely up. Dad brushed past him and making his way around the damage went out through the still open front door to meet them, Alan close at heel. Eric came loping around the side corner from the back veranda, ears pricked up at the disturbance out front, and seeing Alan there came and stood behind him, shaking, licking his nose and teeth bared.

"Bit 'o fun last night, Mr Cameron?" the sergeant called across, his face split in a smirk too obvious to go unnoticed. "Thought we'd call around and see if there's anything we could do to help. No complaints?"

"What? No, no complaints. Just an accident, you can see, foot slipped off the clutch."

"Sure about that? We have your Mr Andy Yatjimarra in the lockup, drunk and disorderly. One fuck of a hangover right now. Anything you'd like to add?"

"Like what?"

"Like, serving liquor to an intoxicated person."

"No, mate, sorry, Andy was intoxicated when he got here, and he was denied service. As he left, apparently his footed slipped and his vehicle came through the window. Then he left on foot, disappeared somewhere. We have at least five witnesses. We're cleaning up the damage, as you can see. No worries, eh?"

"These are the only premises in Ballard licenced to serve alcohol."

"Well, yes, but that doesn't mean it's the only place you can get it. We are on a main road, cars and trucks coming through here all the time. We are not responsible for that. We can't be held responsible for that, sergeant. It's not something we can do anything about. That's your job."

The sergeant stared hard at him for a long moment, then glanced quickly down at Alan, and then at the dog, and turned brusquely on his heel and got into the patrol car. His constable got in the driver's side, slammed the door and started the engine, and then spinning the wheel turned about sending red pea-gravel and dust flying, and they left.

"What do you reckon?" Stan turned to the two brothers standing behind them.

"Got 'im. Prick. Odds-on they're the ones who fed Andy the piss." Dan said quietly.

"What are they on about, do you think?"

"Wants the licence. That's Jack Hanley. His old man owned the Settler's Arms, remember? That's 'is mate Ted Morwell owns the road house. Got no money. When 'is missus pissed off back to Perth she hung 'im out to dry, and 'e's got nothin' to retire on. So 'e wants the pub."

"He can get a pub anywhere he wants. Why here?"

"Ah, well, old Jack, you know, 'e's a bit of a zealot. Mad cunt. Got tossed out of the SAS and joined the coppers. Political connections, eh? So they sent 'im out 'ere as border patrol, out of the way, out of trouble, keepin' an eye out for the bikies comin' through

46

from over east, 'n starlings 'n sparrows 'n fuckin' kookaburras, if we knew the rest."

"Nothin' better to do, so 'e's givin' you the shits like 'e did the last bloke. Reckons you'll pack up an' leave too, and 'e'll get the licence finally."

Alan stepped back away from the two uncles slightly, looking up at them.

"How do you know all that?" he wanted to know, head cocked thoughtfully to one side.

"Well, sis - yer Mum - went ter PLC with Madge Williams. They were best mates. Madge is married to Jock Graham, Assistant Commissioner. Silly cunt doesn't know who 'e's dealin' with. 'E'll be right."

They all turned and went back inside. Before long Bunna arrived in his truck, and backing up to the Toyota got out and tied a chain around the back bumper. Climbing back up into the cab he slowly and carefully dragged the old ute back out through the window and off the veranda.

The men stood around inspecting the damage, which wasn't great once they started cleaning up, and decided among themselves to simply board it up for the moment, and make up a story to tell the customers and make it into a bit of a laugh, a bit of folklore, and she'll be right.

Nothing to do now, at least until 10 o'clock when he had to do the banking, Alan wandered off back to the house.

Eddie was there dragging a mattress into his room, and when he appeared said to him to give him a hand with it. He walked around him to look into his room, to find his things moved across to one side, and a bed frame and chest of drawers there against the far wall.

"What are you doing? That's my room."

"Ah, no good you by yourself. I sleep your room now. Keep an eye on you, eh? This one big room, plenty room, no worry."

"Why do you need to keep an eye on me?"

"You marry sister me. Mother looking after sister, can't be with you - too young you mob - but you mother father not looking after you, same way. You whitefella, *Katepa* fella, don't get it. No good you by yourself. Too lonely for you. Anyway not safe for you, not now. Copper cunt coming after you, coming after dog, coming after Andy, no good. Fucking cunt, all right, 'elp me bloody mattress."

That night after cornet practice for some reason Alan decided to take a shower instead of a bath. It was something that came back to him often over the years. At the time he wasn't thinking about anything much, but he did later. Eddie came in and casually undressed, leaving his clothes and underpants on the floor. There was no shower curtain or privacy. He turned to look at him, then down at himself, and then back again.

"What you lookin' at?"

"Nothing. Just thinking."

"What you thinkin' about?"

He turned to face him directly. "Your father," he said, taking a breath, "said to me you told him I have a good body, that I'm a good person, not rubbish, like, he trusts your opinion, I mean, about me and Gracie. But you're still a boy just like me, the same."

Eddie just looked at him, ears cocked, listening.

"What you mean?"

"What I mean is, why me and not you? You have a good body too, for a 12 years old, nice looking, and real smart. If I had a sister like you, and a father like you, I would say to my father that Eddie will make her a good husband."

"I read about it. Exchange sisters. Not just to protect them, but to look after each other. The man's job is to protect the family. To protect the family a man must be strong and healthy. Is that what you're saying to me? Is that what you mean?"

Eddie stared at him for a long moment, then taking his towel from the rack held it out to him, and stepping under the running shower with his other hand pushed him out.

"No worries, boss," he said. "You got no sister. T'is pella got 'im promise girl 'long Walilya Siding. Can't see that girl, no good me. You look after yourself, eh? You owe me one."

When they were both in bed, after the lights out, he turned over in the dark and said, "All right, Eduard, you're so smart, what's the real reason you're sleeping with me in my room?"

After a long pause Eddie said, "That uncle mob b'long you over in sleepout, that two brother b'long mother side aunty b'long me, tell me move in 'ere. That Andy Yatjimarra, uncle, drunken bastard, pick 'im up cop station, lockup, they gotta look after 'im properly, stay with them in that sleepout, make 'im work, stay off that grog. No place for boys. That mother side one, that Alice, move in my room in 'ouse. Move out demountable 'ouse, live with sister. No room for kids."

"What about Gracie? What is she going to do?"

"Ah, no worry, women's bijnitch, orright? Go to sleep now, eh?"

"But you haven't answered my question yet. Why my room, and not the spare room? Why aren't you in the sleepout with Dan and Harry? Need to keep an eye on me, really, is it?"

"Yeah, that's right. You clever fella properly. No good lonely. Promised boy wait for growin' up, wait for girlfriend like me, no jiggy-jig, too lonely."

Eddie turned over in his bed, glancing out the window across to the back of the pub. "Those two brother uncle just there, look, close up we," he said. "Single men's bijnitch, this side b'long pub, 'ouse; 'nother side women's bijnitch. All fella same, single men, no kids to raise. Tomorrow we go ride 'im 'orse, find sugarbag. Orright? No worry, go sleep now, she'll be right."

But he didn't sleep. He was an only child, a city boy with busy parents. This was all new to him, to be considered instead one with other boys and with men, facing life's realities way out here in the desert, and he lay awhile thinking about it.

PART TWO

Chapter Ten

"Alan, you ride that brown gelding, all right?" Dan said softly, out of earshot. "He'll be quiet, 'till you find your seat, eh?"

"You'll have to show me what to do."

"Not a lot to it, son. Just go steady. In the wild a horse is naturally a prey animal, you need to remember that. They're like cattle, or sheep are worse; they see bogeymen everywhere. Take the lead, let them know what you want, and don't do anything to spook them."

Dan spoke softly as he walked in and took a bridle down from a nail where it was hanging next to the stall. "Here is your bridle, pretty simple, see, head piece and brow band at the top, nose band and bit at the bottom. These connecting straps are called cheek pieces, and the strap under there is the throat lash."

"OK, now hold the head piece in one hand and put it up over his ears. As you're doing that, with your other hand make sure the bit goes into his mouth, and he's comfortable with it. Then do up the throat lash, and Bob's yer uncle."

"Lead 'im out now, and ties the reins to that post."

"Now, this saddle we use is called an Australian stock saddle. It differs from the English saddle; mainly it has knee and thigh pads each side, where the English saddle has a knee roll down the front of the flap. Notice that it doesn't have a horn like the American saddle. That part is called the pommel, then the seat, then the back part is called the cantle, and underneath at the back is what we call the back panel. Both sides are your flaps, and down them are the stirrup leathers and stirrups."

"Oh yeah, OK, that's easy. What are those little brass Ds and things for?"

"You're right. Those front ones are called staples, and under there is the stirrup bar that the leathers are hanging from. Hang your water bag off them, or your saddle bags, or rifle scabbard, what you want. Take that blanket there now, and put it over the horse's back. Talk to 'im, pat 'im a bit, so 'e follows what you want. Talk quietly, see; watch 'is ears flick back listening to you".

"All right, yeah, that's good. Straighten it up a bit, eh, and I'll put the saddle on for you. Reach under there and grab the girth strap for me, and buckle it up here. Pull it tight. Look out, bastard this one, see, 'e's taken a big breath and holding 'is chest out. Reason 'e does that is because once we've done up the girth 'e's more comfortable, but it will be too loose and you'll fall off."

The horse was stubborn and held his breath, so Dan punched him sharply just behind the ribs and quickly pulled the girth strap tight before the horse could draw in another breath.

"And don't take any bullshit from them, all right? Here, stand here son, and I'll give you a leg up."

Once in the saddle Dan adjusted the stirrup leathers for him, measuring his leg length, and seeing his feet were properly in the stirrups. Then he went in and brought his own horse out and saddled up.

All mounted and ready, he sat watching Eddie for a moment. "Any bullshit from you, Eddie, fuckin' hooligan you can be sometimes, I'll give you a good larrupin'. You look after Alan, all right. Ride steady, don't try and be a smart cunt."

Eddie turned away, hiding his grin.

"Look at me, you little shit. What did I say?"

The other snapped his head around, eyes bright, looking Dan directly in the eye. "You said, no bullshit. Don't be smart arse. Look after that fella. Ride steady. No worries, all right. I good fella, look after 'im properly. Don' worry so much."

"All right, go on then. You know where we're going', you lead off. Go on, off you go."

That night Alan was in a lot of pain, his inner thighs chafed raw. After a long shower he gingerly dried his body then sat on his towel on the bed, legs splayed wide apart; head down applying a thick greasy liniment given to him by Sam that filled the room with the rich scents of cajuput oil, cedarwood oil, and citronella.

Eddie sat on his own bed opposite, watching, curiously detached.

"Wrong trousers, unna," he said finally. He stood and rummaged through his belongings, and from a suitcase took out an old clean pair of soft moleskins for him to wear.

"Alan, you wear this one now. Better for you. Sorry 'bout that."

"You should be." Alan looked up. "Next time Dan really will give you a thrashing. I'll do it myself, fuck it, Eddie. Watch out, you're not so bloody smart. Maybe you'll beat me but I'll hurt you while you're doing it, hurt you real bad don't think I fuckin' won't, bloody kill you; make you seriously think twice, next time."

Eddie simply nodded, almost to himself.

"No worries," is all he said. "You're all right, Alan. You can take it. Just makin' sure, orright."

Chapter Eleven

It was late May, coming into early June, and way out here while the days were still hot and Alan got about in shirtsleeves, at night it was freezing cold.

Eddie was right. At that end of the front of the house, across from the sleepout, mid-morning it was warm and sunny and the two uncles, waking up after their late nights at the bar wandered over with their cups of tea and sat there sunning themselves.

By then he had finished tidying the bar and done the bottleshop and the float for the day's till, and came and sat with them. Eddie always appeared alongside him on cue, from whatever Sam had him doing. They had their schoolwork in for the term and nobody to chastise them, and he had the banking ready the moment Mrs Robinson came and opened up.

Putting down their cups of tea, one or other of the brothers would pick up a piece of leather, and with his pocket knife and from somewhere an awl and needle and thread began to repair a bridle, or a piece of saddle; yarning between themselves in the sun while the boys sat watching.

Harry always seemed to have spare pieces of leather. Sometimes he would come riding in with a kangaroo over the saddle, and there'd be steak on the menu, and kangaroo tail soup, then a week or so later he'd emerge from behind the meat house with a whole, newly tanned hide that he'd done with salt and tea leaves, or some tree bark that he'd collected, depending on the colour.

One morning he called Alan over to give him a hand. He just wanted him to hold one end while he worked, trimming off the daggy bits around the edge until more or less satisfied with the shape, he picked up another tool and began cutting lacing from it, bending to work around and around in the one continuous strip while he motioned for Alan to simply follow him about and hold the sheet of leather steady for him. Coming into the centre, he stood and trimmed it off leaving only a small round piece which he gave to him. Then he turned and taking Alan by the arm turned him around and still saying nothing roughly measured his waist.

Andy standing with his axe over by the woodheap had stopped to watch by this time, then came across. Close behind appeared Bunna. Harry was standing there running the new lacing through his fingers, pulling it straight, then deftly measured it off and cut it into 6-8 lengths and folded them all in half.

Without noticing that everyone had gone quiet, Alan watched fascinated as Harry sat down and began work; holding the lacing across his knee creating a start pattern then swiftly started to plait, repeating the pattern all the way down.

Andy was the first to break the silence. As if from a trance he turned to gaze bleary-eyed at Alan sitting there across from him.

"That 'Arry uncle you fella, boss, 'e plurry champion," he said quietly, "plaiting champion, puckim legendary. Belt, stock-whip, ev'ryt'ing. Make 'im you kangaroo belt, stockman's belt. No worry, eh? You like us now, properly."

They all turned casually to look at him, and he went quiet. But he'd pricked Alan's curiosity.

"Is that for me? A belt?"

"Ah, you earned it, Alan," Dan said. "You're a good lad, got balls. You're a trier, that's what we want."

Alan cocked his head, thinking. "I didn't do anything."

"It's not what you do, son," Bunna interrupted, "it's the way you do it. You're good, we can see. That fuckin' Eddie gave you a fuckin' hard time that you didn't deserve, but you stood up to it, showed him you're better than he is, and taught 'im somethin'. That and a few other things."

Alan frowned slightly, and unable to think of anything to say turned to watch Harry at work. It was like somebody playing an instrument, totally absorbed in the task, concentration palpable as the new belt grew under his nimble fingers, stopping occasionally to stretch and straighten it, and work it, until eventually he stopped suddenly and leaned forward to rifle through his kit. He came up with a pair of solid brass rings, and slipping them over the working end began to weave the end lacings back and tie in the loose ends.

The thing was beautiful. The rich red-browns of the tan shone in the morning sunlight, set off by the shining brass rings.

Alan stood and went to go inside. "Get my moleskins," he said, almost off-hand. "My shorts aren't much good, it'll look better."

"Nah, you'll be right Alan," Dan said. "Sorted. Come here, son, stand here. You too Eddie."

He reached behind him and brought out two parcels wrapped in plain brown paper. Undoing them he laid out new moleskins, and shirts, and R. M. Williams dress boots, indicating for the two boys to undress, no bullshit, everything, you're men now.

Standing there naked, the men passed them new underpants; proper cotton Jockey Y-fronts not children's nylon town briefs, new socks and shirts and trousers and boots, until fully dressed Harry stood to give Alan his new plaited belt. He took out a second belt he'd made and passed it across to Eddie. Properly dressed now, the men stood and gathered around them.

"All right, now, you two fellas," Bunna started. "No more bullshit. You are men now. Alan, when you marry Gracie, and you have your kids, this brother-in-law belonging to you will be their uncle, properly, mother's side. You need to understand that."

"Eddie, this brother-in-law belonging to you will be their father. You need to respect that. No more bullshit. You are men. All those

57

kids coming along need a good father, and a good mother, and a good uncle and aunty, all the way up, all right."

He stopped, watching their faces.

Alan cocked his head, thinking, then glanced back at him, and Bunna gave him the go-ahead to speak.

"If that's right, well, Eddie says he has a promise up at Walilya Siding. That means she is my sister, that girl, right? What's her name?"

Bunna glanced sideways at Andy, then looked up again. "Ah, that's Andy's niece, his sister's daughter, but other side, Warmunya side; father belong real desert mob out the other way."

He leaned back, half-turning, and tossing his head indicated the general direction.

Alan turned to look at Andy. "That's why you're here, isn't it," he said, "keeping an eye on things. I was wondering about you mob. Veronica's here because she's married to Sam, his father; Gracie's father, but her sister Alice doesn't need to be here, she's just hanging about. So are you, Andy, just hanging about. No kids of your own. So why are you here? Because Eddie is here, is that right? He's your investment, isn't he?"

At that moment Dad came out through the back door, dressed and ready to start opening the bar. He glanced across at Alan and everyone gathered there, and Alan picked up his clothes and turned to go back inside to change out of his new clothes, and do the banking and help him.

"Yeah, all right, no worries," he called back. "Just give me a tick, I have to work, help Dad. I know now; what's going on. Thanks, trust me. It'll be right, OK?"

Inside, he took off his new clothes and folding them put them tidily away, but then on second thought stepped back into the new cotton Y-fronts, and took the old soft pair of moleskins Eddie had given him, and buttoning up an old short-sleeved shirt he pulled the soft moleskins on, then the new belt to hold them up, then last of all his old shoes and socks. He looked at himself in the mirror.

As he went out the front door and steeped across to the hotel, the men turned to watch him.

Andy grinned, "Properly!"

Chapter Twelve

Ten minutes later Alan came back out and called across, "Ah, Uncle Dan, Dad says the glass is here for the front window, and some wood, and window frames. And there's a heap of pipes and stuff, and bags of cement, and paint and stuff."

"Right you are, lad," Dan called back, and the men stood and started packing their gear.

He was coming out of the bank with the float for the day's till, and they were all there now at the front of the hotel, going through the new delivery all stacked on pallets that must have been dropped off by one of the trucks passing through during the night. Even Sam was there.

As he came back along the veranda toward them Dad was putting a **BAR CLOSED** sign up, and he asked him what he wanted him to do with the float.

"Put it in the till, son. How much have you got?"

"Fifty dollars."

"Yeah, it'll be right. Fifty bucks won't hurt. Just put it in the till, eh? Then come and give us a hand; working bee today, get this show back on the road. What do you reckon?"

"Yeah, all right, good. I'll get changed if you like."

"No, don't worry, you'll be right as you are."

He looked around. "What are all those steel pipes for?"

"Bollards. We're installing bollards. Insurance."

"Really? What's Andy doing with the shovel? He's not doing all that by himself, is he?"

"No, he just has to dig the holes, and mix the cement. That's his punishment. He knows, he'll be right. Give me a hand with the invoices."

"But Dad," he said, frowning now. "That wasn't his fault. That police sergeant, if you're right, he's the one who should be being punished."

Everybody stopped to look at him.

"I don't understand," he went on. "Why is Andy being punished? Dad, he's not like that; you used the wrong word, now I'm confused. Why are you saying things like that to me? If it's about right and wrong, and being punished, it's the police who are wrong, getting him drunk like that. He's a good man, he just didn't know. It was you who was right not letting him have any more."

"What are you talking about, Alan?"

"What? What am I talking about? I don't know. What are you talking about?"

"Well, that's just the way it is."

"What? No. No it's not. What's the way it is? What does that mean?"

There was a long silence, everyone watching him.

"Sorry Dad, but," he was watching Andy. "Well, the way it is, is Andy is Eddie's father-in-law, but desert side. Properly, I should call him father, looking after me. You should call him brother. He is your brother. That's right. Mum is Alice's sister, but far enough away, so it gets sorted out, so I can marry Gracie and it's all right for me, but Andy is still father belong me. You should call him brother. I'm not wrong, am I?"

"Sorry, Dad, all I really mean is, I'll help Andy. Better for two men to be digging holes, it's a bit of a job for one man by himself. I'll help him dig the holes, is that OK?"

Stan glanced down at him and nodded, then shrugged and without saying anything went over to the pallets and started removing the invoices from their plastic stick-on envelopes.

Alan was to think a very great deal about that conversation later, but at the time he felt he was in the right. It had been a good morning and looked like being an even better day, not imagining how it would end.

The day itself went well. When Dan and Harry boarded up the hole in the wall after Andy had crashed his ute through it, they'd cleaned up all the old bricks; scraping off the 120 year-old lime and sand mortar and stacking them all neatly along the side of the building. Taking the boarding down they quickly tidied up while Bunna laid out some old sheets of iron and began to mix up a new batch of mortar for them.

Sam had Eddie painting the steel posts with rust-proofing - heavy 6" bore casing - while he and Andy set to work digging holes. The ground wasn't hard, mostly sandy loam, gravelly at the top where over the years people had surface dressed the ground for parking. But the holes had to be a good 3" deep, and they had to bend to the task. It was hot work. As Eddie finished painting the first of the steel bollards Bunna mixed some cement for them; a harder mix with blue metal in it, then set out a string line and set the first of them in place.

He was impressed at how well organised they were, at how well the men's teamwork flowed; each taking a turn at giving another a hand, none of them saying much at all. Once the brickwork was done, while Eddie continued painting the bollards Sam went across to help the two uncles start on the woodwork. When Eddie was done, he sauntered over and started on the next hole.

Just after noon Mum brought them all lunch, fresh sandwiches and cups of tea, then they all started again and were finished by 4:30 and Dad re-opened the bar.

They all decided to knock off. Eddie and Sam could come back tomorrow to finish painting. They were all tired, off-guard, not paying much attention the way they should have been. The bar wasn't busy and Dad had sent Dan and Harry off, so after a normal dinner in the kitchen they all retired.

The early customers stayed away, however, calling by during mid-morning to find the bar was closed and men working, and not bothering to come back. A couple of them bought cartons from the bottleshop through the side door, and stayed home to drink it.

Not long after 11:00 pm Alan was awakened suddenly by a cry from the back of the hotel, and sounds of struggle followed by running footsteps. Eddie was awake too, and quickly out of bed. They pulled on some pants and ran outside to see what happened. Dan and Harry were there already. Dad was lying across the septic tank with blood streaming down his face, his old brown school-case carrying the day's bar takings gone. He rolled over and struggled to get up, holding a broken arm, casting about for the brown case.

He stood and staggered about cursing and muttering, oblivious to the people gathering around him.

He called out in the general direction, "Gutless bastards! Bloody deadshits. Eighty bucks, eh? Picked the wrong night, eh? Come Saturday you'd have got three and a half grand. Eighty bucks! Dumb-arse stupid pricks, how dumb can you get? Fucking unbelievable!"

But Mum was there too now, talking to him, and people had hold of him, calming him down, until finally he turned and refocused, unsteady on his feet.

There was a gash down his forehead, running from the crown of his head to his eyebrows, and blood in his eyes and running down his nose and chin. A steel jemmy was on the ground where it had been dropped. He'd put his arm up to protect himself from the blow, so instead of caving in his skull too deeply it had cut him, and broken one of the bones in his forearm.

They sat him down again on the septic tank while Mum ran inside for the First Aid kit. When she came back Stan fought her off, not letting anyone near him, until eventually Eddie ran off to get Sam, and Bunna appeared, and got everyone else to stand back.

Slowly he began talking to him, as a soldier wounded in the war, coming quietly onto him and giving him clear orders until Sam arrived, and in the same officer's commanding voice soon had him sitting quietly, receiving treatment.

Chapter Thirteen

The police line-up were all blokes from the roadhouse, and their mates; the blokes who came in early in the day for a beer and unemployed nothing else much to do. The two men who attacked him were complete strangers, and no effort had been made to round up anybody else apart from the few locals. The one he was looking for, who belted him with the jemmy bar, had brown hair with a thin weasel face, while his offsider who'd grabbed the school-case was wearing a hoodie, and what he saw of his face was unfamiliar.

Stan turned to the sergeant, saying nothing.

"Eighty dollars, is that all, Mr Cameron? Doesn't seem much for a busy hotel. Are you sure the amount stolen is correct?"

"I already told you, we do banking at 9:00 o'clock for the breakfasts, and late bar and dinner; Alan does that, and the late banking at 4:00 for the day trade and lunch, which Elsie does. We're empty, no more buses until Friday, for the weekend. We scheduled the work in a quiet period."

"So, how much would you ordinarily expect?"

"Eh? You want me to tell you that, in front of these blokes? That's confidential, I wouldn't even tell you. You know better than to ask such a question. It's none of your business, is it?"

"Well, just trying to help, Mr Cameron. Anything else we can do for you?"

"Don't think so, no. I've lodged my complaint. Let's know if you catch those fellas. Can I go now?"

The sergeant simply shrugged, not letting go his gaze, or the lingering smirk, then stood aside. The constable looked on, face set, grim.

65

Outside in the tiny foyer of the rough, demountable police station Elsie and Alan got up from their seats and followed him out.

On the way to the car Stan kept saying, 'sorry love but I just can't handle that sort of bullshit,' and he'd turn to Alan saying, 'I'm your father, son, nobody else', and back to Elsie again with, 'we are a good family, they're supposed to be protecting us', and to nobody in particular, 'the bastard wants the bloody liquor license, does he, over my dead body' . . . and muttering to himself.

Alan opened the passenger side door of the station wagon for him and he got in, while Elsie went around to the driver's side and Alan got in the back. His Dad was scaring him, and he sat watching him brows furrowed, eyes bright all the way home.

He didn't sleep at all well that night.

At dawn next morning as he made his way sleepily across to the hotel, through the corner of his eye he caught a shadow against one of the elegant Salmon Gums across from the kitchen that for some reason didn't seem to belong there. It was odd, there was one of the dining chairs tipped over, and he went across to pick it up and bring it inside.

It wasn't until he drew closer that something made him look up. Maybe it was the polished shoes and pressed trouser cuffs that caught his eye, there in the dim half-light; anyway that was the image that stuck in his mind. It wasn't Dad's bloated face staring down at him from up there somewhere, with the sticking plaster on his forehead, but the neatly pressed neat cuffs and clean shoes. Dad must have bent down and wiped the dust off them.

It was like him to do something like that; so typical, so familiar.

It was odd because they were up off the ground; there was no clean carpet beneath them, and he couldn't get an idea of what happened to the carpet to register.

Before he could think much further a shrill scream split the air and he turned to see Veronica running toward him. He didn't remember anything else.

When he woke Mum was sitting on his bed, stoking his brow. She'd been crying. Eddie was sitting watchfully on his own bed. Bunna was standing next to the door, and next to him at the end of Eddie's bed Sam stood, patiently waiting for something, or so it looked like. As he sat up they all snapped around to look at him.

"What's happening?" He gazed about, disoriented, then without thinking turned and picked up his watch.

"Ah, shit, look at the time. What are you all doing here? Sorry, ah, I don't know, I must have slept in. I didn't mean it. Hell, Dad's going to kill me, the bar'll be a mess. Sorry everyone, I . . . what? Why are you looking at me like that?"

Sam came over and took his pulse, then took his face in his hands and looked into his eyes. With one thumb he drew up his left eyelid then after a quick glance let it go, and turned to speak quietly to his Mum.

Alan sat there, trying to think.

"What's happening with Gracie?" he said. "I saw Veronica. She was upset. Are they all right?"

"Ah, they're going up to Lake Marnma, Alan," Bunna said. "Gracie's going to school up there. No good here. It has nothing to do with you, like, she needs her singing lessons."

"Oh well, that's all right. Good. Gracie, she has this really great voice. Mum's been doing a good job with her, but she needs to go further. Sorry to say, Mum, I mean it, really, I don't think you're not a good teacher, but, like Sam taught me something else, that Gracie already knew, but at the same time she does need the technical skills. Will Nanna be teaching her?"

"Why are you looking at me like that?"

Nobody said anything. He sat back, still trying to think.

Nothing was making any sense.

Mum was staring at him. Her lipped trembled and she looked away, then she started crying.

He looked up.

"I didn't mean it like that. I know, Gracie was really happy."

"It's all right, son. It's not your fault. Have a rest and we'll call in later to see how you are. It must be hard, I know. Do you want Sam to give you something, Alan? Will you be all right?"

He looked at her, but then she stood suddenly and taking a glass of water or something gave it to him, and he leaned forward to drink. It was foul, like Sam had soaked his dirty socks in warm water, but with a pleasant soft lemon aftertaste. He closed his eyes and drank it all down at once. Glass empty his Mum took it from him and left. He watched her leave. After a long silent pause Sam followed her out, and then with a quick side glance at Eddie Bunna left too.

Eddie sat listening, not looking at him, then the moment it was apparent the grown-ups had gone he stood and went out onto the veranda. Holding it open for long enough to let Eric in, he came back inside. While the pup leapt onto Alan's bed, tail wagging, he sat back on his own bed.

Alan held Eric close, patting him and sniffing his fur while it licked his face, then he lay back. Gazing up at the ceiling, one hand holding the dog and the other idly scratching his forehead, he said finally, "My Dad's dead, isn't he."

Eddie sat quietly, not answering.

"Why did Veronica take Gracie up to Lake Marnma? When did they go?"

"*Mapun* 'ere now. No good this place. People frighten. What you talkin' 'bout?"

"When did they go?"

"Just this morning. Hour or so. She'll be right, no worries, eh?"

Chapter Fourteen

In the shock of the moment nobody had thought to notify the police. Mrs Robinson instead called Kalgoorlie when she arrived to open the bank and Post Office, and they immediately despatched a car to accompany the coroner's anonymous white panel van, though they would take over 3 ½ hours to get here.

Sergeant Hanley was incendiary. Ten minutes later, having been notified by Kalgoorlie of the death by radio, he arrived in the white patrol car in a cloud of dust and flying gravel. He stamped around for a long drawn-out moment until he spied the rope-end dangling from the tall Salmon Gum just over from the kitchen and he strode across. He looked up, then turned gazing about.

Somebody cocked their head in the direction of the house, and he strode across there and went inside through the front door. Stan was in the makeshift schoolroom inside the house where he'd been laid out straight on the front desk, with a clean sheet over him. He went in and pulling the sheet aside made a quick inspection before nodding and striding back out.

Walking back past he poked his head through the open door into the boys' room where Alan was sleeping off the valerian and lemon balm Sam had given him, the red pup curled up on the bed next to him. Eddie looked up, face frozen, while the pup bared its teeth in a frightened snarl.

The sergeant simply snorted, then disappeared out the front door and strode directly across to the hotel. There was nobody in the kitchen so he made his way down the passage to the front bar where Elsie was sitting quietly head to head with her brothers. They turned to see who it was.

"Good morning, Mrs Cameron. Mind if I come in?"

"Sergeant Hanley?" she sat looking at him, then shrugged resignedly. "Well, you're in, aren't you? What can I do for you?"

"You have an unreported death on the premises. I'm here to investigate."

"I'm sure you're mistaken. The death of my husband has been reported. The police are on their way, with the coroner's people."

He stood staring at her for a long moment, taken aback.

"I am the police, Mrs Cameron. Why wasn't this reported to me?"

"No, I'm sorry, what are you talking about? People here are in state of shock. Mrs Robinson was kind enough to notify the appropriate authorities. Is there anything I can do for you?"

He stood, shaking his head as if trying to clear his thoughts. He turned and walked around the bar, stopping to run his hand along the counter, and his gaze along the racks of clean glasses and shelves of bottles. Eventually he turned to the three of them sitting there, and said carefully.

"I'm afraid you will have to hand over the keys, Mrs Cameron. I'm closing the hotel pending further enquiries."

"Enquiries? Would you care to tell us what enquiries?"

"Death of the licensee, trading without a license, for starters."

"I'm sure you're mistaken. As you can see, we are not trading. The bar is plainly closed. I am the nominated licensee. It was my husband and bar manager who died."

He crossed to the front door and looked up, and read from the plaque. "Licensee, Mingellia Holdings Pty Ltd trading as The Ballard Hotel, nominee E. S. Cameron - that's Edward Stanley Cameron. I am aware that the deceased is Edward Stanley Cameron."

"I beg your pardon, Sergeant Hanley. I am the registered license nominee of this hotel. I am E. S. Cameron; Elsie Selena Cameron. I can prove that to be the case. My brothers here are both registered barmen, and licenced security personnel. The company in which we hold significant shares has been notified of events. They are kept routinely up to date, and have been made fully aware of the circumstances in which we find ourselves. We are in good hands, I assure you, and will in due course reopen the bar."

The sergeant stopped suddenly, face reddening, then snapped his head about abruptly staring at her. He turned on his heel and stormed out. Halfway along the passage his footsteps stopped and he came back, poking his head through the door.

"A word of advice if I may, Mrs Cameron. There is a large contingent of motor bike riders, criminal elements, making their way across from Adelaide. We are on full alert. It is my job to protect you. You wouldn't want to get caught up in any sort of trouble, would you?"

Elsie gazed steadily at him. "I'm certain we're safe, Sergeant. Thank you, I'm sure, for your concern. I promise, if we need your assistance one of us will call you directly."

An hour later they were still sitting there, only Bunna poking his head in in the meantime to let them know Alan was asleep, that Eddie was with him. As he spoke from a distance began a deep-throated roar that slowly increased in intensity until it became painfully deafening and the front windows rattled, before it went silent; the only sound the ticking of hot engines cooling.

There was a knocking at the front door, and Dan went over to open it. "Sorry, we're closed," he started say, but stopped suddenly, eyes wide, and turned to Elsie.

"Sis, you won't believe who's just rocked up."

She cocked her head at him and he stood aside. A rough dirty looking bloke came in wearing soiled jeans and black boots, and leathers and club colours over a filthy t-shirt.

She stared at him, until recognition dawned.

"Well, look who it is. Dougie Ryan. I don't believe it. How many years has it been?"

"G'day Else," he said. "'Ow yer goin', love? Ah, we 'eard you was 'avin' a bit o' trouble wiv some copper out this way. Some idiot cunt; Jack fuckin' 'Anley, they say. Thought we'd ride out 'n 'ave a look at 'im. Orright wiv you, is it? Orright if we camp over the way there, like?"

Chapter Fifteen

The day turned out to be anything but ordinary. As the long line of bikers started up, amid the shattering roar of open exhausts they rode across under the tall elegant trees to scatter the goats and claim their patch. They were all still waiting in the bar for the coroner to arrive when Alan woken by the din came in with Eddie, and Harry pulled some chairs over so they could sit with them.

By then Monique had the kitchen open and making a bistro lunch for everyone of crunchy sliced baguettes with *pâté de foie gras*, *camembert* and sliced olives with a crisp salad of Sam's fresh garden vegetables, liberally doused with her own tangy *vinaigrette*, and a carafe of young *vin de maison* grapella trucked across as backload from Rosa Glen.

When the police arrived with the coroner's people finally it was just in time for lunch. They'd picked up Veronica and Alice with Gracie in tow out on the road, hitch-hiking, but the women refused to leave the car so Bunna took food and drinks out to them, not saying anything to them and they said nothing to him either. They weren't there.

After lunch as they stepped outside the big superintendent sent his senior sergeant over to the biker's camp for a quiet chat, but when he turned around Andy was standing there at the end of the veranda.

He gazed curiously across at him, cocking his head.

"Andy? How yer goin' mate? What are you doing in these parts?"

"Orright, boss. Just keepin' eye on things, unna."

"That cousin of yours in hospital belong Kal, tell me, tell 'im that Andy fella, orright."

"O' yeah. T'ank you, boss. You tell 'im that fella, orright, orright."

74

"All right, I'll do that."

He paused a moment, then glanced toward the car.

"That missus belong you, sister-in-law, that little girl belong your mob, eh?"

"That right, boss. Not s'posed to be 'ere. Should be Lake Marnma. No good 'ere, t'is place."

"Is that right? What's wrong this place? What's going on?"

"Ah, no good, boss. Properly dead fella 'ere now, that one b'long missus." His eyes rolled in fright. "*Mapun*, no good. Missus b'long me clear out, go Lake Marnma. Take 'im that little girl school, properly."

The super thought for a moment, gazing about.

"We give 'im a lift, eh? Drive 'im Lake Marnma. Not far out of our way, you'll be right."

"Ah, t'ank you, boss. You good pella b'long our mob, no worries, eh. That mob there, tell 'im, orright. Tell 'im, we go Walilya, take 'im two boys b'long that sister-in-law, b'long missus. You tell 'im, orright."

"No worries, Andy. You good fella, no worry me. Look after you, all right."

Then he turned on his heel, looking at Alan and Eddie, sizing them up. He turned to Elsie.

"Elsie, all right, love, let's get this job done. Sorry to keep you; it's not easy, I know."

"That's all right, Bob. Way out here . . ." she nodded almost to herself.

"Boy's all right, are they?"

"Yes, they're all right."

75

He turned his gaze back to Alan.

"Son, Alan is it? We need you to testify, all right. Alan, we need to conduct a formal coronial hearing into your father's death, and we need to cross-examine you. Might as well do it here. We can do it in the Post Office, Mrs Robinson knows what to do. I do need to know whether you are OK about it, up to it."

Alan gazed at him, frowning slightly as he glanced away into some far middle distance of his own, then back again.

"Yes, it's all right. I'm all right. What you want me to do is all right."

"Good lad. Just stand there a minute, will you."

He turned again and strode back to the car, and opening the front door sat sideways in the seat to turn back to talk quietly to Veronica, arm casually over the backrest, motioning with one hand as he spoke to her. Finally she nodded too.

The big police superintendent then rose and without further ado directed his sergeant to come with him, and the coroner's men to come too. They all disappeared around the end of the veranda toward the tree with the cut rope still dangling from the lower branch, and the nice clean dining room chair with the high-arched back and floral seat still lying there strangely out-of-place in the brown dust beneath it.

The hearing was cursory, almost. It took up no more than half an hour or so from the time they started setting up the back room of the Post Office, which turned out to be the old mining claims tribunal with an ancient carved wooden bench on a raised dais at one end that could be entered through a side door. All they had to do was bring in some chairs and a table, and shift a stack of cardboard cartons out of the way that looked as if they held over a century of Ballard archives.

Mum was the main witness, telling them about how Dad hadn't been sleeping very well since he'd been mugged, getting up at night and pacing around, and that she'd been taking sedatives in order to get some sleep herself. She had no idea that Stan had dressed and gone out so early.

She thought he might have suffered some sort of concussion, deranging his thoughts, as he'd kept pacing about murmuring soundlessly to other people he imagined around him, as if he were out on patrol in the desert; an old war trauma triggering anxiety and disorienting him from where he was.

All Alan had to do was answer questions Yes or No, about whether it was his father he saw hanging there, but unable to think very clearly himself simply nodded Yes to everything. So had Veronica in her turn.

When it came to the difficult part, and he was asked whether he thought somebody else might have murdered his father, and made it look like a suicide, he looked up and shook his head.

"No," he said. "Because Dad wiped his shoes clean. He was always neat and tidy. If there was somebody there trying to hurt him, his shoes would have been dirty. He wouldn't have let them; he was a soldier, you know, he would have fought them, and his shoes would have been dirty."

The coroner's man turned to the super, asking him if there was anything he needed, but he was gazing intently at Alan and needed prompting.

"Ah, no, thanks André. That'll be it," he said quietly. "We're satisfied there was no foul play, not directly at least. We only need to ascertain the cause of death. We can let these people go, if you will, they've been through enough."

After they all filed out the two officers and the two coroner's men sat talking the matter over a while longer, before one of them poked his head through the dividing door politely thanking Mrs Robinson, and they all packed and left. The white panel van quickly drove off so they could be back in Kalgoorlie before knock-off time, while the super glanced at his watch and made his way along the veranda to book a room for the night.

That done they returned to their car and drove over to the local police station for a second, internal police enquiry.

Chapter Sixteen

After a good long shower and change into civvies followed by a meal in the dining room, Bob went down to the bar for a quiet beer. After they'd finished late talking to Hanley and the local constable he'd sent his own sergeant out to Lake Marnma to drop the girls off, and stay there the night for a bit of a look around while he remained in Ballard. He'd drive back and pick him up in the morning.

He paid for his beer, Harry making no effort to refuse him; good man, honest pub. He glanced about. Nice and clean, some of the fittings a bit old but heritage building. Tourist minibus in for the night, with couples at the bar talking and chuckling among themselves.

Alan and an old Chinese guy in the far corner across what passed for a lounge were playing blues, subdued, on a sad note but not maudlin, not at all unpleasant. There was a drum kit there on the raised platform, and a piano. An idea for later.

As he turned further gazing about around Elsie in the other corner caught his eye, and he went over. She was sitting there with Dougie Ryan, still in his colours, and another huge bloke as ugly as sin.

"Who's your mate, Doug," he wanted to know.

"Ah, that's Barry, Bob. Barry Devlin."

Barry stared impassively, until Doug turned to him. "Mate, we 'ave the honour and pleasure of the company of Superintendent Bob Kelly, boss cocky for the entire Goldfields. We all go back a long way, me 'n Bob, don't we, Else?"

Bob allowed a slight smile out the corner of his mouth, not taking his eyes off Barry, cocking his head slightly at the compliment.

"Bad Barry, isn't it? How long have you been out?"

"Out 'a where, Bob?"

"Pentridge."

Dougie turned to his mate. "Ah, mate, don't bullshit with Bob Kelly, eh? 'E's orright. Knows everything, does Bob."

"Yeah, well, two weeks. Thought I'd come for a bit of a ride. With the fellas."

Doug was watching Bob's face. "Rehabilitation, Bob. Settlin' 'im back into the community, ye know what it's like, eh."

But Bob wasn't listening. "Explosives, was it?"

The table fell silent, until Elsie learned forward and said, "Bob Kelly, you behave yourself this minute. You're off duty, and this is my party. You too, Doug."

She turned to face Barry, apologising, "Old school friends, Barry. Please excuse us. We were all in the same class at school, as thick as thieves, and here we are. What in Heaven's name has brought the three of us here together I'll never know, but By God I'm going to enjoy it. This is going to be a wake we'll never forget."

Doug grinned, eyes distant, then nodded and leaned forward, "Yeah, that's right. She was the boy, so she got 'Else' not 'Elsie', isn't that right? Trouble was, then she come back from Europe all doozied up and pretendin' to be a lady."

They all fell silent again, looking back. Finally Bob said to her quietly, "That's when you met Stan, wasn't it, love? Met him on the plane coming in from Singapore, remember?"

She looked at him, and replied almost inaudibly, "Yes, I remember."

She turned in her chair at that and said out loud, "Harry, be a love and close the bar for me, will you? I'm sorry, ladies and gentlemen,

I'm sure you understand. My husband has died, and this is a private party. If you would like to stay on, please feel welcome."

Standing, she said to Bob and Dougie, "Help me bring him in, will you. I don't want him out there by himself. Find Bunna, somebody, he knows where things are. There must be a gurney or something around the place."

Instead of a gurney somebody found a food trolley from the dining room, and wheeling it out the back found an old door and placed it on top.

Alan followed them out, asking, "What are you doing, Mum?"

"A bit of a send-off, what do you reckon?" she said. "We'll send him off happy, like the old days. He'd like that."

"Are we going to have a funeral?"

"In the morning. The cemetery is just over the side there, toward the roadhouse. Don't worry about it now, all right. Would you like to give me a hand with him?"

He stood holding her hand for a long moment, holding her back; holding her to him, then he nodded finally to himself. Bob was standing next to them by then, looking down at him.

"You OK, son? Do you understand what we want to do? It's traditional, a wake, to celebrate your father's life. Your Mum wants him to be there with us, and we can bury him in the morning. You can play for us, play for your Dad, you're something of a celebrity, I hear."

"Do you mean, Last Post? Tomorrow?"

"Sure, yes, if you want. That'd be nice. Tonight we can just play music, and enjoy ourselves. Is that all right?"

"Do you play?"

"Sure, drums. Friend Dougie there plays banjo, guitar, if he's got them with him. Your Mum plays piano, we'll be right."

"Sam has a guitar."

"So, all right with you? Do it?"

"Yes, OK, it's OK. What do you want me to do?"

"Ah, give us a hand with your Dad, is that all right? We have to move him onto the gurney so we can wheel him across. We can lay him out on the pool table if you like."

It took around half an hour to get things organised. Mum went off to help Monique with food while the men rearranged the seating in the bar and lounge.

Alan almost unconsciously took careful control of moving his father. He wasn't happy about moving him; it wasn't quite what he'd been thinking about, and refused to allow anybody to show the least disrespect. It was a good thing he was neatly dressed ready to open the bar for the day, with freshly pressed shirt and trousers and shoes so shinily polished. It passed through his mind for a protracted worrying moment that if they had to change him he would object, but they didn't.

Once he had spread a clean white linen tablecloth over the pool table and they carefully laid him out, he spent some time arranging his collar; pulling it up higher and tucking the chafed skin of his neck under, to make it look nicer. Somebody had pulled his eyelids down shut, sometime or other; must have been this morning while he was out. He took two new dollar coins from the till and put them over his eyes, leaning over to straighten them like he'd seen in the movies, and then stood back looking at him.

His Mum was standing just behind him by then, to one side, and she draped one arm across his shoulders causing him to look up. She was crying.

He took her hand, murmuring, "It's all right, Mum, he won't be worrying any more."

"It's all right for you, son," she said, somewhat abruptly, surprising him. "You have only lost your father. I've lost my lover. What am I going to do now?"

He was lost for words, astonished; what she had said unimaginable, but before he had time to think of something to say to her Bob was there.

The party was soon under way, though Alan only played for a short while before seeing Eddie at the door watching him, and he took his chance to leave. He was sad, he felt sad, the party was artificially happy, and seeing his dad lying there dead only this morning with so much happening during the day, and such a big day yesterday, nothing seemed to register.

Sam was watching his face, then nodded and waved him away, go, it's all right, Eddie looking after you.

The two boys made their way up the passage past the busy kitchen and across to the house. Eddie was trying to talk to him but he wasn't listening. He simply turned to him with a confused, distracted look on his face, so Eddie kept quiet after that.

Inside the house he was unsettled. He kept getting up and walking around, sitting for a while on the front desk where his Dad had lain all day, then for some reason he couldn't explain went into his parent's bedroom to poke around, trying to make contact, maybe. There was a battered old tin trunk in the bottom of the wardrobe and he remembered his Dad carrying it, sometime, enough to pique his curiosity, so he pulled it out and opened it.

At first sight it was just a collection of old books, some not so old but well-thumbed. On top was a book with the title, *How to Win Friends and Influence People*, by someone called Dale Carnegie, then another on *The Art of the Rhetoric*. Beneath them was a cloth-covered manual from the army on self-defence and unarmed combat, and another like it on firearms and rifle range drill among another pile of books on accounting and business management, hotel and bar management.

Picking through them he found a nice, well-kept copy of *The Rubáiyát of Omar Khayyám* by Edward FitzGerald, then when he picked it up underneath it was a hard cover book on health and family planning, with pictures of nude people, and children and genitals, and couples making love, and another one by Steve Biddulph called *Raising Boys*, but then beneath that again he dug out something else called *The Kama Sutra*.

Lost in the contents of the trunk he squatted there leafing through it, gazing at the pictures. He could feel an erection and absently reached down to fondle himself.

"No good like 'o dat. Don't do that, no good," Eddie said almost into his ear, and he jumped with a start. "You promise sister belong me."

Eddie was standing over him and he glanced up quickly then back at the book. He closed it, and went to put it back but on second thought he stood, then bending over took out some of the books he wanted to keep and put the rest back. He shoved the tin trunk back into the wardrobe.

Eddie was watching him. "What you want that for. Shame, that business, no good."

"No, it's all right. They belonged to my father."

He looked him in the face for a moment, then said, "I'm good. I'll be good. I love your sister, I don't hurt your sister, Eddie. You don't have to worry about me, all right."

"What you goin' to do with them books?"

"They are mine. I'll take them with me. It's none of your business."

Half pushing him aside he went back to their room and put the books in the bottom draw of his bedside chest. Eddie followed him in but he didn't want to be talking to him. Instead he began to undress for his shower, until fully naked he stood unabashed and pushing his way past Eddie again went into the bathroom and turned on the shower, leaving the door open. Eddie could suit himself.

Eddie followed suit a few minutes later, and stood patiently waiting his turn.

Chapter Seventeen

They'd found a coffin. There was a stock of them in the shed over behind the roadhouse in case of road trauma emergency, for the most part. It was plain, but nicely finished and Dad wouldn't mind. Mum must have brought up the coat and vest that went with his nicely pressed trousers, so now he was in his suit with the lid still off and his army medals across his chest.

People were watching him as he came up with Eddie in tow, but he didn't look for long, only running his hand along the coffin's lip while he glanced at his face. His cheeks were sunken, and there was a grey pallor to his skin, but that was all right too because he knew now that his father was dead, and that's what dead people look like. He had his books, they were his to keep, and he was the man in the family, and whatever else he didn't want to be thinking about; not right now.

The police superintendent was in full uniform, with his service medals across his left breast, and so were Bunna and Sam in suits with their medals. Mum looked all right. They'd been up all night but she'd been home for a shower and a clean-up, and to wake the boys and have them up and dressed.

There was no minister. Bunna did most of the talking, mainly about service in the military and men's bravery, and what happens to men, to their minds and ways of thinking, and settling back into civilian life. Then Bob stepped up and with a quick glance at Alan spoke of his father's own service, and for his benefit explained what each of his medals represented; first above the others his Group Citation for Bravery, given among men showing great bravery together, followed by his personal medals; his Star of Gallantry, Distinguished Service Cross, Distinguished Service Medal, Active Service Medal, and lastly because he was a fine shot with a pistol his Champion Shots Medal.

Then Bob spoke of Stan Cameron the man, and how glad his wife's old school mates had been that she'd found such a good decent bloke. He was a quiet, self-effacing bloke who kept a lot to himself, who should have been awarded the Victoria Cross though he hadn't pressed the point, or allowed anyone to argue on his behalf. Alan glanced up to see if the big policeman was having a lend of him, but his face was calm. That was before their son was born, he went on, after a few good years of happy marriage followed by war service in the Gulf. Mum was watching his face too by then.

After that Bunna stepped forward and unpinned the medals, and making his way around the coffin pinned them onto Alan's right breast before turning around to fit the lid. And the four men lowered it into the ground. Andy came up suddenly daubed in white ochre, dancing around them as the coffin disappeared, then sat and began to wail. Nobody told him to be quiet.

As the earth was being shovelled into the grave Bunna turned to Alan, giving him a quick nudge, and he raised his cornet to his lips and played the Last Post, this time blowing his soul into the brief refrain making everyone turn to listen. For some reason his eye caught the big ugly biker standing at the end of the grave, Bad Barry or somebody. As he played, suddenly he saw Barry's left eye pop out, and a tiny gush of blood spray before dripping down his cheek. His eye was hanging down, dangling from the optic nerve. More blood trickled from his nose. Nobody saw what was happening since the men had stopped shovelling dirt to listen to him playing, and were looking his way.

Barry sank in slow motion to his knees, taking forever it seemed, until a sharp crack rang out as if from a long distance. Alan was playing his cornet, just finishing the final notes; in his mind and his breathing counting more than two seconds, about 2 ½ seconds. By then Barry was falling forward. Nobody else knew anything until they heard the shot and saw Barry already tumbling head first into the grave, but by then Sam had hold of him pulling him down, and Bunna was on top of Eddie and Bob had grabbed Mum and everyone else seemed to have just disappeared.

There was no sound for long minutes, only breathing and after a while somebody coughing and spitting. There was a siren wailing, and tires screeching, and as they slowly rose the white and blue patrol car went speeding past along the main road, toward where the shot came from.

But instead of racing past the hotel turnoff where the patrol car should have been at that speed came a great blinding flash of white then yellow and red and orange flame and the car just wasn't there anymore, and the siren wasn't wailing anymore, but instead came a gigantic roar and shock that sat them all down again.

Bob was up first. Alan would remember the look on his face, as if to say, right, we're on, but glancing across at Dougie he only got a bewildered shrug that made him stop in confusion, and look around. Nothing.

Dan stepped quickly through the tangled mass around the grave to grab Alan by the arm, then Eddie with his other hand, and ran them both together back over to the house.

Andy had already bolted.

Chapter Eighteen

The two boys were kept hidden under the front desk in the schoolroom for what seemed to them hours, the red pup loyally with them, taking turns to crawl across to the front window to look out and see if they could see what might be going on, when after only around 40 minutes Dan rode up with a string of horses all saddled and ready to go.

He dismounted and strode purposefully into the house, and as they rose to greet him he said, somewhat brusquely, "You boys need to clear out. Andy will take you up to Walilya Siding, out of harm's way. We don't know what's happening here yet."

Alan started to tell him where he thought the shot might have come from but he pulled him up short, telling him to pack the things he'll need, with warm clothes and spare jumpers because it's nearly June and cold in the desert at night, and oilskins because it might rain.

Eddie jumped promptly to it, raised in the desert and not having much to carry anyway, but Alan had his belongings, and all this was happening way too fast. He went into the kitchen and digging around in the drawers found a roll of gladwrap. Back in his room he carefully took all his books and wrapped each of them around and around in the thin cling film and packed them all in a clean pillow case.

He stood for a moment, thinking, then crossed to his parent's room and reaching up onto the top of the wardrobe took down his father's old swag, and dragging it back unrolled it and placed the books inside before rolling it back up again and doing up the straps. He put his cornet case and trumpet case on top, then stripped out of his clean funeral clothes to dress in moleskins and shirt. Taking a soft case he packed spare clothes, and jumpers and t-shirts and placed that on the pile too.

Dan stood watching him, before stepping back outside and calling across to Andy to bring up a second pack horse.

Done finally, they led the horses across to the kitchen where Mum and Monique had cooked food packed and ready, and supplies to last a week or more if necessary which they packed in the saddle bags and cases slung over the first packhorse. She went to kiss him goodbye but he held back, and she looked at him and after a short pause nodded. He was a grown man now, that boy, grown too soon, but she said nothing.

They simply mounted and rode off.

Riding past the huge crater in the main road, Alan pulled his horse across to speak to Bob Kelly.

"Um, excuse me, sir, but you should listen. Where that shot came from, I think I know."

The big policeman turned to him and stepped over. "What is it, son?"

"Well, um, none of you were watching him, looking that way, like, when that Barry took the bullet. I mean, where I was standing, looking the other way, if you line up Dad's grave that way, it came from there. I was playing, counting my time, and it was 2 ½ seconds. The sound took 2 ½ seconds, if you know what I mean, from the time he was hit. I was thinking about it. At the speed of sound, you know, if it took 2 ½ seconds, I reckon 850 metres. If you trace that line 850 metres straight from my Dad's grave, I bet that's where the sniper was."

"You sure?"

"Yes, I'm certain. I saw it. The bullet didn't come out. Look at Barry, there is no exit hole; just his eye, like, pushed out, you know. But there will be a hole in the back of his head. I bet. Have a look.

You can get the bullet out and look at it. Maybe there will be a cartridge case over there."

The policeman turned his head to gaze in the direction Alan indicated, then back again.

"Good work, Alan. I'll get you a commendation for that. Now you'd better clear out, this place will be swarming within the next hour or so. We don't even know if the area is safe yet, or what else might happen."

Alan continued to sit there and the policeman glanced back up at him.

"Who was in the car? Just that sergeant; just him?"

"Yes, how did you know?"

"Well, I didn't, I just guessed. He'd be right. Think about it, he was up to something, about the hotel, setting something up, but he stuffed things up and they got him."

"Who? Do you have something else to tell us? Come out with it, eh?"

"What? No, I'm just guessing. I'm only a kid, but kids aren't stupid; kids see things. It makes sense, that's all. Put it together, and think about it, and it makes sense. I know about the bullet, I saw it, but this, I mean, I can't say I know it just makes sense is all."

Bob stood there frowning, but then instead of replying to Alan he simply nodded and glancing across at Andy said, "All right, you'd better clear out. It's going to be very busy here before long. How long, Andy, do you reckon?"

"Maybe, week, boss. We'll be right."

"All right. We'll radio ahead to let them know when to expect you."

Then he turned back to Alan. "Son, don't say anything to anybody. Keep your mouth shut, do you understand? You'll be safe with Andy. Once you get past the old 17 Mile, past the minesite; that's his country after that. He'll take you to Walilya, you'll be safe there. Officially you are still home schooling. We'll sort the rest out later."

"T'ank you, boss." Andy was calling back. "Tell 'im, orright. One week, eh?"

Without ado Andy spurred his mount and took off at an easy canter. Alan had no chance to respond when his horse simply turned about to follow, unbalancing him and causing him to hang on while the red pup loped easily along at heel. The super stood gazing after them.

Fifty minutes later, out along the old mine road heading north, as they broached the lip of the scarp they looked back down to see helicopters coming in low from the west, and vehicles on the main road converging at speed.

Once they crossed over and were out of sight they settled into a steady walking pace, making their way down through much rougher country off the scarp. At the old 17 mile peg there was a dry creek bed with a derelict wooden bridge across it. They were down on the flat by this time, with the rough back side of the broken scarp now behind them. Across the old bridge, instead of continuing along the same track heading northeast Andy left the road and bore northerly along the east bank of the creek.

This country still had a scant covering of mulga with the occasional quandong with ripe red fruit that could be seen from a distance, and rough grass breaking up into clumps of spinifex. It was much easier riding here and they made good progress, though it was starting to get late and they would soon have to stop and camp.

Alan spurred his mount forward a little.

"Andy," he wanted to know. "Why would that policeman tell me to keep my mouth shut? I wasn't thinking about saying anything to anybody."

"Don' know, boss. Maybe up to somethin'."

"Andy, don't call me boss, all right."

"You're right, no worries. Son b'long me. That other one son-in-law b'long me. Go Walilya, orright. Properly. Sit down time, little bit. You'll be right."

"Yes, all right, but you didn't answer my question."

"P'lice bijnitch. No blackfella bijnitch. No worries, orright."

"What that old man means, Alan," Eddie broke in, "is don't ask so many questions. Rude to ask questions. That one, father-in-law belong me, call 'im Yatjimarra. Proper Law Man. No more Andy, all right. Andy just gammon name, town drunk name, whitefella business."

"How are we supposed to learn anything, then?"

"Just be quiet, and listen eh? Whitefella can't listen. Now you belong blackfella way, learn to listen. Don't ask question . . . look out . . . all right?"

He was about to ask another question when Eddie spurred his horse and rode on ahead. There was a bend in the dry creek bed and he pulled up there.

The first thing Alan was to learn was to not camp in a dry creek bed. Once they made a small camp for themselves and set a fire, Eddie led him down onto the sandy bed and showed him how to dig for water, and use that for the time being since they'd need the water on their pack saddles later, once they were into the desert proper. While he was doing that he showed him which grass to use, to form into a mat to filter the muddy water while he leaned forward to sip directly from the hole in the sandy creek bed.

The same soft grass, he went on, was the soft one for wiping your backside after you've taken a dump, and while talking to him about that took a stick and dug a small hole in the ground a bit away from the camp, and squatting over it acted out the process before filling it back in. Once into the desert there was only the interminable sharp spinifex, and use a round stone instead if you could find one, or in a hurry clean sand. Alan soon realised there was going to be a lot of showing and acting out on this trip, and sitting listening, and looking, and not much talking.

The second thing he was to learn was to respect Yatjimarra, respect the elder - they were travelling through his country now - and do the jobs that needed to be done neatly and straight away, always keeping the camp in good order, and as they went on their way not leave a mess behind.

The soft insides of his thighs and up under his scrotum where he sat in the saddle were OK, not as bad as he thought they might be. While Eddie hobbled the horses to prevent them from straying far, following a quick inspection he rubbed Sam's balm on only a couple of small spots before pulling his underpants and trousers back up.

That was it. Eddie cooked a fairly simple meal which they ate quietly while it was still light, before rolling out their swags and the moment it was dark went straight to sleep.

Dan had been right. Out here in the open it was deathly cold, in the small hours. Hearing him restless and teeth chattering, despite Eric snuggled up against him, Andy spoke quietly across to Eddie who got up and covered him with some extra blankets, and they didn't stir after that until small birds flitting among the low mulga branches began to twitter and twerp in the pale early light of dawn.

There was dew on the ground, and fresh green grass coming through. Eric brought in a rabbit and they cooked it on the fire for breakfast, Eddie still making porridge for them while boiling a billie for tea. As they sat eating Yatjimarra looked on with approval while Alan fed Eric bits of cooked rabbit, who sat happily at his feet and looked as if ready to go get another one except Alan spoke and said sit, and scratched his ears him with his free hand. Their meal soon out of the way Eddie started cleaning up, and leaving Alan to wash the plates and things with wet sand and silty water in the creek bed he went off to bring the hobbled horses in.

When Eddie came back with the horses he said quietly that another rider had passed through, only yesterday, maybe yesterday morning, riding at a canter.

Horses saddled and packed they headed off straight away. Quickly Eddie showed Yatjimarra the fresh tracks. There had been no tracks on the road or across the bridge. The rider must have crossed over the scarp down the other end away from the roadhouse, where it was more difficult but out of sight of the buildings, then ridden across country until he encountered the dry creek up ahead and turned to follow it.

They were both looking at Alan by then.

"The fella b'long you mob, Home Lake mob, Alan." Yatjimarra said softly. "That one uncle b'long you, mother's brother, two uncle brother. That one Uncle Ken Forrestal b'long you. Good shot, that fella, properly. State champion."

Chapter Nineteen

Around mid-morning they stopped to rest the horses. Eric went off again somewhere, and Eddie made a small fire to boil the billie and make tea.

Both of them were still watching Alan closely, attentive to him, but annoyed and distracted he kept brushing them off.

Eventually Eddie said to him, "No good for you, Alan, no crying. Why you not crying? Your daddy finished, everything buggered up. Can't cry, make you sick."

He stared at him, eye's glistening. "You told me not to ask questions, all right, so I'm not. I'll sort it out myself."

"Not like that. No good like that. What you want to know?"

"Nothing. I mean, what next? What else do you know about my family that I don't know? I never had anybody telling me anything, just busy all the time. Now all this. I'm not a bad person, why don't people just talk to me, tell me things?"

"Ah, you'll be right. You're a good fella. We like you. Look after you, all right."

"That's not what I meant! And anyway, what about my Dad? I don't even know if he's got a family, or who they are."

The two glanced at each other, trying to think, until Yatjimarra said something to Eddie in the language, turning to indicate a long way east.

"He said, b'long Sydeny side, that mob. Your father people not from here, over east. We don't know that mob."

"What about Home Lake mob? What about them? What's going to happen next?"

"Nothing, Alan. Don't worry. Can't talk like that. *Mapun* listening. All too quick, frighten. We go Walilya Siding, sit down

96

time you, all right. After that, maybe go Home Lake. Your mother family there. You cry now. No good can't cry, make you sick; make us worry for you."

He stood looking away for a long moment, then mounted up and taking the long reins of the two pack horses softly whistled to Eric, and rode away.

Eddie called after him, "Not that way. Go 'nother way. We show you, all right?"

Alan pulled the horses up and without turning around sat waiting for them. Eddie tidied up the small cuppa tea camp and they too quickly mounted their horses and rode on. As they made their past Alan gently spurred his horse and followed.

They went on like that day after day. He didn't want them to see him crying, though as they rode along the tears streamed down his cheeks and they didn't say anything. They all stopped for dinner, then again mid-afternoon for smoko, and made camp at night when they had their dinner mainly steak and onions with damper and fresh fruit, and breakfast early the next morning before starting out again. No matter what, they washed everything down with black tea sweetened with sugar.

Eric brought in rabbit most mornings and they cooked it the same, and he shared it with him along with slices of cold-cut beef and pieces of fresh damper, and he let him lap water from his own cup. Sometimes he lapped up the last of the tea as well, and at night nosed his way under the blankets and crawled in underneath to snuggle next to him, and he was glad of it.

As they started coming up out of the sparse mulga and up into more broken country, finding quandongs Alan stopped to pick some and eat them, then dismounting tied his horse to a loose branch and went for a walk, Eric at heel, while the others waited patiently for him. They had to keep moving, that was all. There were rock wallabies up in there too, and once they started out again Yatjimarra began telling stories about them, and about country, so for the rest of the way he simply rode along quietly listening.

Toward the end of day six, by then far out across the vast treeless plain where they seriously needed old Yatjimarra or become confused and lost with no landmarks to guide them, they heard a cry up ahead; somebody calling out to them and they rode closer. Somebody was waiting there for them. They must have been there for a day or more because their camp was settled and well organised.

There were a couple of old men there, sitting calmly watching them come up, both with bright red wool wrapped around their heads, and a younger man and some boys about the same age as he and Eddie. As he glanced across at him he noticed Eddie's head down, looking away in awe and respect. The younger man was speaking in language with Yatjimarra.

Eddie edged his horse in closer to Alan and said to him quietly, "This one fella granny belong me, name Francis Patjarli Miller, call him Frank Miller, all right? He proper big boss this place. 'Nother granny belong you, father belong Andy Yatjimarra, call him Boniface MacKenzie. You call him Boniface, all right. Don't talk to that old man Frank, he father-in-law belong you. This other fella talking now, he Yatjimarra cousin, father side, call him Teddy Scott."

By then the men had stopped speaking and were looking at the boys. Teddy nodded briefly at Eddie indicating they should dismount, and as they did so he stepped across and shook hands. He took Alan's hand and led him over to the two old men, and he politely shook hands with them in turn before introducing him to the boys, his tribal brothers brought out from Walilya community to welcome him and escort him in.

The introductions out of the way the old man Frank simply stood and without saying anything walked off toward the northwest. Eddie remounted and without saying anything either rode off after him, leading the one pack horse carrying most of their food and water, and leaving the other with Alan and Andy and his mob.

Chapter Twenty

There was a polite knock on the front door as he sat eating breakfast, and the house girl went to answer it. It was the local constable. The house he'd slept in belonged to the Baxter's, the school headmaster, and they were sitting in the kitchen. The boys had dropped him off there last night once they rode in, and left his two saddles with their saddle bags, and swag and instrument cases on the front porch before taking the horses away somewhere to be groomed and fed.

Eric during the night had pulled one of the saddle blankets down off the rail and made it his own. As the front door opened to admit the policeman he started in behind him, tailing wagging, but Alan simply told him to stay and he turned and went back out again.

"G'day, Alan. Alan, isn't it," the constable said, friendly and relaxed, causing Alan to warm to him straight away. He nodded.

"I'm Constable Grant, Tim Grant. Just calling to see that you got in OK; some letters for you. Don't mind if I sit? How are things, all right? How was the trip?"

He sat easily and comfortably, and the headmaster leaned over with the teapot and filled him a cup.

Alan was looking away momentarily. "Yes, thanks, I'm all right. We had a good trip, it's not too bad really. I thought the desert might be a lot harder than that. Bit cold though, in the night. And I know I can ride now, so that's good."

By then Tim had passed his letters across to him and he sat leafing through them. There was one from Mum, and another from the Education Department with his term results, and the last one in an ill-formed hand that he realised after a moment was Gracie's. He checked the postmark and it was from Lake Marnma, so he tucked it back under the others. He understood now that she'd be frightened for him, crying for him, and he'd get word to her later to say he was all right, arrived Walilya all right, no worries.

On second thought he opened the second envelope and taking out the official sheets passed them across to Mr Baxter who glanced through them and smiled, then nodded before showing them to the constable. Alan eyed him warily, not expecting the courtesy.

"Bright boy. Welcome to Walilya. You'll be an asset. Play footie?"

"Yes. Back pocket, half-back flank mostly. I can play forward as well."

"That Eddie can play. Wing, rover, very fast. What's he up to? Seen him around?"

"Ah, he went off somewhere with his grandfather. They didn't say."

Jim Baxter interrupted, wanting to know which way they went. Alan had to stop and think, and reorient himself to the new place, finally indicating northwest.

"They'll be out at Kurrkutja, at the outstation. Bush holiday time," the headmaster said. "Frank will have a few of his boys out there for law business. If you want to see Eddie, he'll be out there, otherwise better to wait until they're finished; 2-3 weeks."

"No worries. He's here all right, that's all I need to worry about."

Tim turned back to Alan. "You OK, Alan? Anything you want to talk about? Must have been nasty."

He stared at him for a long moment then shook his head. "I'm all right. Don't worry. I miss my Dad, that's all. That Bad Barry bloke got shot and fell over. His eye popped out and he fell over, then the patrol car went up. Jeez, did it go up, BANG! Hell, it just blew up. It just wasn't there anymore. There was this great ball of fire, and we were pushed over, but I don't know anything after that. We just, sort of, ran over to the house, and that's all I know. Except, when we rode past there later there was this great big hole in the road, and bits of car everywhere. The engine was, shit I couldn't believe it, like, 100 metres away. Hell. I sure remember that."

"Wow, that's what happened? That's it? Pretty scary. Didn't see anything else, anything on the way here? Nothing to add?"

"What? On the way here? No, nothing. I didn't see anything. I don't know. Maybe you should talk to Andy, or Eddie, I wouldn't know. Bob Kelly was there, he's your boss isn't he, ask him. I don't want to talk about it, anyway. I was missing my Dad, really bad, that's all; it's only a week, and I just . . ."

"No worries, Alan. We understand. Call in at the clinic later for a check-up, will you? Let the doctor have a look at you, eh?"

"Yes, I will, that's all right. Tell Mum I'm here OK, will you? Tell Bob Kelly I got here OK. I can't think of anything else."

"Sure, no worries. What do you want to do now? You want to stay here with Mr Baxter? We have a dormitory of sorts for the boys in from the desert, mainly Andy's mob. You can stay there if you like, it's a nice tight little community, so long as we know where you are."

"We'll sort that a bit later, Tim," the headmaster said. "There's no rush. Mr and Mrs Forrestal are driving across from Lake Marnma; his grandparents. They'll be here soon. We can all have a chat then, when we're all here."

The constable drained his cup and stood, taking his leave. Alan gazed after him.

"He's all right," Mr Baxter said, reading his face. "This is a good community, very close and supportive. Tim's the footie coach, mostly. We're a sort of frontier outpost. Out there are the real desert people, and back that way are the mines and goldfields and all the bullshit."

"It's all right. What do you want me to do?"

"Well, you're welcome to stay here with us if you want to, Alan. Plenty of room. But, if you want my opinion I think it would be good for you to join the boys in the dormitory. It's not so much a dormitory, but we call it that. From what I hear, you're promised to Grace Cheong. Don't worry, we are fully briefed on that business. What I mean is, that Andy Yatjimarra, you call him father, and Eddie Cheong brother-in-law. Everything works by kinship. Most of those boys over in the dormitory call you brother. Eddie's promise, that girl out at Warburton, they call sister."

Alan sat staring off into space, then turned his head to look at him again.

"I mean, sorry, what do you want me to do?"

"Ah, yes, Alan, you can do a lot of good out here. These people are terrified of the whitefella, for good reason. You can help them, be their friend, give them confidence. You're a fine student, I saw your grades. So are these boys, a lot of them, and should be aiming to enter university, not just desert law way but both ways. If you can help . . ."

But Alan was watching the frustration in his face, and short on patience he leaned forward.

"It's all right, I've got it. No worries. I'll be good. Anyone play guitar, or flute, or didj? Can we get some music happening? I can play footie, and I can ride too now. The horses are mine, aren't they, from Home Lake? We'll be right."

The headmaster merely gazed at him a moment and said nothing, then went back to finishing breakfast. As he rose from the table and gathered his plates, he said, "Alan, when you finish be a good lad and go and see the doctor. We need to give you a thorough check-up, not just for your own health but to establish your incoming medical baseline. In the dormitory, be careful to keep to yourself and keep yourself clean. Is that all right? Dr Jayaraman is very good, she will let you know the rules. By then your grandparents will be here, and we can talk things over then."

He simply nodded. His breakfast was cold so he let it go, draining his tea instead. As he was about to tidy up the house girl was there taking things from him, pushing him with a shy smile out the door.

Outside Eric was immediately there at his heel as he stepped out onto the dusty common; like Ballard passing for a main road but without the hard black strip of tarmac running through it, and without the goats. The trees were different here too, desert ghost gums in place of the elegant tall Salmon Gums, though not much else. A mob of children in place of the goats ran across jostling and calling out to him, "Alan, you name Alan. Alan. Alan. Alan. You name Alan, eh? Papa. Papa b'long you, eh? Tis pella papa, red dog papa, b'long you. Alan. Alan, eh? 'Ome Lake. Stockman, properly. You stockman, eh? We ride 'im 'orse. Me me me me, no me firs. Alan. Alan. Ride 'im 'orse, eh? No me firs. Take me. Me. Me. No me. Alan. Alan. Alan. Alan."

He wasn't to realise until much later that he'd arrived on horseback with their senior tribal elder, leading a packhorse, dressed in desert-stained moleskins and shirt and hat, wearing a Harry Forrestal plaited belt and an Akubra hat, and R. M. Williams boots, with a red half-dingo pup at heel that they all called him after, or that that was the children's full impression of him; not some green wet city boy who played sweet cornet, and ran the hotel bottleshop, and did the till and the banking, and read books, something entirely foreign to them.

He didn't have to ask the way to the clinic. Somehow or other the surge of swarming children simply washed him up there, depositing him there like an ocean wave stranding a sea shell on a beach before retreating back into the surf. He went inside and was met by a very nice lady with jet black hair and evenly tanned skin who didn't look at all aboriginal, who he guessed must be Dr Jayaraman. When he went in and took his clothes off she called after him that he could keep his underpants on, but he looked down at himself and said it doesn't matter, I'm not that shy.

She gave him a thorough going over, even having him turn around and bend over, and cough, and taking a plastic stick with a swab on the end from a sealed plastic tube rubbed the inside of his cheek with it and put it back. She sat him down and straightening his arm carefully inserted a needle into his arm, inside of his elbow, and attaching a series of syringes took what seemed an enormous amount of blood, five of them altogether.

Almost absently she said to him he could get dressed now, but with at least his underpants back on sat him down again to ask him questions.

He'd never taken much in the way of medicine, only Panadol elixir when he was little, and all the vaccines, and Dr Zhang's valerian and lemon balm after Dad died, and his liniment when he came in from riding the first time with chafed thighs. He spread his legs wide apart and showed her the old chafe marks from riding, but she was far more interested in how he was feeling now about his father, and sitting back watching his face anything else he had on his mind.

He glanced across at her, but didn't say anything aside from that there was some stuff but he was OK about it; family things. Then he stopped and stared out the window, and looked back at her again, but still said, "No, it's all right. I'll be all right."

She gazed at him for a moment, then nodded to herself.

"All right, Alan," she said finally, "you can get dressed now."

Then she said, "Alan, you are a very intelligent boy. Just so you know, we have a full team out here. Open collaboration is very important. Ordinarily we would be sharing information on everyone in the community, but in your case I would like to ask your permission."

He was tucking his shirt in, but he stopped, and looked at her. His eyes glistened, and he said, "Yes, it's all right, I understand. Yatjimarra said, Eddie said, I don't cry, no good for me, make me sick, but, really, I miss my Dad and I'm worried about Mum, and a lot of stuff, but I'm just a kid, really. It's all happening too quick, and I'm promised to Gracie and I want to be with her, ah, you know, sometimes at night it's hard, but I'm good and I behave. No shame, all right. I have nothing to be ashamed of. What I mean is, you know, puberty. I know about, like, sex and things. Sometimes I wet dream, but not a lot. Only a little bit, like, but I don't masturbate or anything. I work hard, and I go to sleep. I don't have anything I want to talk about, especially."

"Is that what you mean?"

She cocked her head his way. "Not quite, Alan, but that's all right. You're a very nice boy, and a brave boy. You are a nice looking boy, and open and honest, and decent. I do envy Gracie. One day you will make her a fine husband, and your children will have a fine father. I'm not worried about you. I also know Dr Zhang, and admire him greatly. But please, if you have anything at all you want to share with somebody, my door is always open."

He was doing his belt up, and bent down to pick up his boots. He sat in the chair next to her pulling on his socks, frowning.

"What is it with people, do you think?" he asked her suddenly.

She looked at him. "Oh well," she said slowly, thoughtfully, after a long moment, "if you do want to know my opinion, the world is full of tragedy. Life is full of suffering. You can read the Hindu Vedas, and the Buddhist scriptures. Read the Bible. Read the *Dao de-jing*. Be learned and scholarly. I am sure Dr Zhang will help you. Keep your focus as a human being, and don't try to work miracles. Work to make things better for others, that's all we need to do in life."

"Do you think so?"

"Yes, I do. I do think so."

"I know Lao-tsu. Sam gave me his *Dao de-jing* to read, and *The Art of War*, and *Journey to the West* and *Romance of the Three Kingdoms*. I brought them with me, with Dad's books. Um, I haven't unwrapped them yet, but I've got them. They're in my swag."

She leaned back in her chair, and smiled, then leaned forward again to complete the form in front of her.

"All right, Alan, off you go then. I'm sure we'll catch up."

Before he left she gave him a handful of health brochures to take away with him, and read.

Back out on the road he ran into the same jostling surging chattering kid mob, all dusky black faces and ivory white smiles, welling back up from some depth onto the same remote beach-head to pick him up and deposit him somewhere else. At the far end of the street a battered dusty Land Cruiser was coming in from the vast expanse of desert, floating in on the heat haze like some sort of blocky, wingless aircraft coming in to land.

As they drew closer he saw it was his Nanna and Pop arriving from Lake Marnma. He broke loose and hurried forward to meet them.

PART THREE

Chapter Twenty One

Mid-January was scorching hot, over 43° for days on end. They had decided to start early, after a good sleep leave after midnight and drive through the early morning to arrive at Wallarabing by around 7:00 am. Anyway they didn't want to be driving all the way back to Perth late afternoon with the sun in their eyes.

Mum had a new station wagon. It was more like a sort of estate wagon, with constant 4-wheel drive and enough room for seven people if they fitted all the seats in the back. She'd had a bull bar fitted at the front with extra driving lights which lit up the road for what seemed miles ahead, but she wouldn't let him drive at night because night driving vision is tricky, out here on the long straight roads, and speed difficult to tell. The new car was so quiet anyway, and the big V6 once they were up into cruising speed just seemed to have taken a big deep breath and run for it.

They were uncomfortable together. It wasn't like it used to be, mother and son taking time out together, to catch up. She wasn't going to put up with his pubescent bullshit, as she called it, but neither was he going to forgive her for rocking up for Christmas arm in arm with Bob Kelly, not without telling him first.

They had argued too about the money Dad left him, over $270,000 that he'd saved up. Before that, he hadn't thought about his Dad living all those years in the hotel, not spending his pay just tucking it away in his superannuation fund and various term deposits. Mum had her share, so he couldn't see what she was arguing about, when he wanted to use his money to buy a house and maybe get some tenants in until he and Gracie were together finally.

Uncle Greg who turned out to be an economist with one of the big merchant banks stepped in and without much ado told his big sister to mind her own flamin' business.

Old Jim hearing of it, trumped them both by turning around and simply giving him the house he still owned in Perth, over in Subiaco, or Nedlands or Cottesloe or somewhere, and telling him to use the equity to buy two houses and get good tenants in them, and keep his money in a good portfolio like his Mum said, and Greg could manage it for him. By God those Forrestals were a bunch. It was as if their whole lives were one endless game of euchre; always out to trump one another, one way or other, with Old Poppie Jim still the reigning champion.

They weren't nasty about it, just endlessly competitive and very clever, and wise, all having a good hearty chuckle over it later. No wonder they were held in such affectionate high regard by the locals.

As they drove through the long night Alan stopped bothering trying to talk to her, and unable to sleep sat back in his seat thinking back over the past 8-9 months of his life.

When Nanna and Pop returned to Lake Marnma back in June they took Eddie and Frank back with them, so Eddie could start school there and get a proper education. His best new friend in the dormitory at Walilya was Reuben Scott. Reuben was a couple of inches taller, and played ruck and centre, and centre forward. In a way Eric introduced them. That pup was crafty, and he smiled to himself as he thought about it. Everyone and everything out there was a wheeler dealer of some sort, nobody was free of the constant scamming and friending, but it turned out well.

Back in the privacy of themselves, back in the dormitory in their own space, those desert boys were a dignified lot. In a way it was a single men's camp. All of them were promised, all of them negotiating puberty, and while there was a lot of chiacking and laughing and boy fun in the end it was deadly serious business; all young hopefuls, young up-and-comers who would be carrying responsibility for their people in years to come.

After they'd all crowded in to look at him, that first night he was in the shower the first time, satisfying their curiosity they relaxed with him and showed him respect. Anyway, he was lucky fella, properly, promised to Gracie Cheong, who they'd all wanted, and something of a pinup girl around the place.

They all cried when he left. Eric had simply trotted across to stand next to Rueben, wet pink tongue lolling, ears pricked up and tail wagging. That Eric wasn't an old man dog, he was a boy dog, and belonged to the dormitory now. No shame that pup, the way it squatted there with its dick poking out like a stick of pink lipstick, panting and dribbling and tail still happily thumping the floor next to it, and he smiled to himself as he thought of it.

It was Christmas at Home Lake that had been really special. They'd all taken a genuine liking to him, having followed his progress and found themselves impressed. Bush people are like that, he could see now. The first thing that happened when he arrived was old Paddie Miller had taken him aside and as everyone looked on rubbed his smelly armpit sweat all over him, and sang over him and cried, then handed him over and sat down again under his tree in the front yard. Old Jim said to him later that it was a rare privilege, now he had proper magic rubbed on him, and he'd be safe in life, wherever he went. He and Paddie as boys had been through the ceremonies, both at the same age he was now, a long time ago, and they were tribal brothers properly. Out of sight of the others he wiped his own armpits and rubbed his rank, greasy old-man's sweat on him too.

Alan noticed often that Jim never talked about anything like that in front of the others, aside from Paddie who only glanced across every now and then with his toothless grin and rheumy old eyes, and never said anything else at all. Confined these days to his wheelchair after such a rough life, his intelligent mind as bright and sharp and clear as an eight year-old's, Poppie Jim always had a way of satisfying everyone, coming up with some way that everyone was a winner; nobody lost out but always gained something in the deal, and with Paddie they sat under the tree through a lot of hours together, none of them saying much, and had their beef and onion soup with bread floating in it brought out to them for lunch.

Great Uncle Harold didn't say much, but he didn't say much to anybody. He met Uncle Ken, who was a geologist and mining engineering consultant to Greg's bank, and came back out here to work cattle in between jobs. One morning at breakfast around the big table in the dining room Ken noticed his nephew looking curiously across at him, but he merely winked and nodded, then turned away and went back to quietly sipping his tea.

Days merged into weeks, broken by Old Jim after dinner wanting constantly to hear him play cornet and trumpet, and in the evenings after Mum arrived with Bob they played, and talked and laughed and were together. It was good. He liked everybody a lot, he just slotted in without fuss, and later on at Bridgefield Grammar when he wanted to be alone there was a good old tree out in front of the chapel where he'd sit for hours on end, the same, and dream blackfella dreams about Old Jim and Paddie, and planning for when he and Gracie would be together.

Back in Ballard a few days ago there was a nice polished granite slab and marble headstone on his Dad's grave, and he picked what he could find of desiccated flower heads, and leaves and dried gumnuts and placed them on top. Over on the other side of the graveyard was another new grave now, with a fair slab and headstone that read simply, Barry Devlin, A Good Bloke, RIP.

What was special was Veronica and Eddie and Gracie back from Lake Marnma. This time he was allowed to talk to her, and go for walks with her, but always with Eddie tailing them except yesterday it was really very hot and he and Eddie were in swimming, she turned up suddenly and promptly slipped off her shift and waded into the other end of the pool in her panties, not looking at him. He had to look away, her breasts were forming and she was lovely. Veronica came up behind her, and moaned and complained and sat on a log under a tree to keep an eye on things.

A bit after sunup Mum pulled over beside the road, needing to pee. He did likewise, next to the road while she went off into the scrub. When she got back he was already in the driver's seat so she let him drive the rest of the way, until a few kilometres out of Wallarabing she made him pull over and change around.

They shared the one room at the motel. He was already hot and stripped for a shower, leaving the door open. He didn't mind his Mum seeing him naked, and anyway he wanted her to know he wasn't a boy any more. But she had grown up with boys and wasn't fussed, being the only girl in a family of men. All she did was glance briefly across, commenting as she unpacked a few of her things merely on his inheriting the Forrestal precocity. When she went in to shower she closed the door.

When she came out drying her hair he was already sound asleep in his cotton Y-fronts on the floor next to the double bed, having dragged the clean quilt off the bed to lie on like that pup of his, and a pillow. She gazed fondly at him, as she was fond of all her men. Gone was his puppy fat, replaced by well-defined abs and pecs, and clear muscle tone in his arms and legs. She leaned forward and brushed an unruly damp lock from his forehead, and sighed.

Chapter Twenty Two

Mum simply dropped him off at the school, and after helping him get his bags out of the wagon briefly held him to her, and tousled his hair and without a word got back in and drove off. She had a job but she didn't mention it to him, so as soon as he was settled he lay down for a nap.

Only later after dinner in the huge school dining room and they were watching television did the penny drop, when the local and regional news came on and she was on it, being interviewed on the historic, heritage-listed Ballard Hotel now owned and controlled by the Kurrkutjatjarra Remote Community Association, and talking about the need to properly control consumption of alcohol in remote areas and ensure sustainable funding was properly directed into education, and outback schooling.

He sat watching with interest; all making sense now, except most of the other boys there were no longer looking at the screen but had turned to stare at him.

"That's your Mum, isn't it?" somebody wanted to know.

"That's you," somebody else said. "You're Alan Cameron. You're the one, aren't you, the cops were looking for. Blew up the police car."

"Boom! Hell, that's you. What did you use? Nitro-glycerine? Blew up the whole road . . . jeez, bits of car were everywhere . . . we saw it . . ."

"Yeah! Boom! Nitro Cameron. That's you. We saw it on the tele . . ."

Voices came at him and at him. The television news channel had moved onto something else, something inane, girls gambolling freely about some paddock covered with flowers, advertising sanitary pads, or tampons, whatever. Bewildered and suddenly angry he stood and walked out.

He didn't know where he was. It was still light outside but he had no direction, didn't know which way the buildings were aligned. Seeing a spreading old tree in the middle of the lawn he simply went over and stood beneath it. Somebody followed him out.

Inside the big hall sharp voices among the shrill cat-calls and chiacking were calling for order. Eventually whoever it was noticed him standing there beneath the tree and came across.

"Are you all right, Alan? Are you OK?"

He shifted closer against the tree trunk while the other continued.

"Alan, I am Mr Carpenter. I am your house Head. Sorry I didn't catch up with you earlier. Bit hectic all day. Come on, come and have a chat, all right? Is that all right?"

"No," Alan said after a long wait. "I'm all right. Don't worry about it."

"Well, yes, except it's my job to worry. That's the reason I'm here. Want to come up later? I'm in my office if you want to drop by. I'm your music teacher too, by the way. I hear tell you're a serious cornet player. You played at the dawn service last April. I was there. I heard you play."

"Did you? Really? It wasn't very good, you know, too technical. I still had to get my breathing sorted properly, relearn a lot of stuff. Do you want to hear what I can play now?"

"Sure. Come up in five or ten minutes if you like, if you need a break. I know, a couple of the boys still need a bit of growing up. We have brought the Year 7s up into senior school through our Primary Academic Extension program to get them started earlier, but it's only the start of the school year. What are you in now, Year

8? Some of the Year 9s and 10s aren't much better. Don't be too worried about them, find your own friends."

When he stepped in a little closer Alan didn't move away, but said, "No, it's all right, I'll come with you. I'll just have to go past my room and get my cornet."

"No worries. You can play for me there if you like."

"I know your grandparents, Alan," he went on as they started walking toward the buildings. "We went through teacher's college together, way back when. They asked me to keep an eye on you. I know your story, you don't have to tell me anything, unless you want to. We have a couple of desert boys here with us, you can hang with them if you like. You'll be a good example, what we need here finally."

But by then Alan had stopped and the other turned to him. He was crying.

"I didn't blow up the police car, I didn't. It wasn't like that. My Dad, um, you know, it was his funeral. It was terrible. We didn't even have a chance to bury him properly. That's not right, I feel terrible about it. If you want to know. I don't want to talk about it. But now you know all right so I don't want to hear any more about it. I'm just a kid, really, I just want to be a kid. I don't want to be a good bloody example, to anyone, just be myself all right."

They stood there for a long moment, not saying anything, out there in the middle of the lawn.

"Alan, I want to say something to you, what your Nanna and Pop and I were discussing. OK? Thing with you is, I know, you have worked all your life. You never did have a childhood, not like these other boys. And now you're betrothed to be married, I know about that too, and I know how seriously you're dealing with it. You're not a child, you can't be. You're a young man too far ahead of his time, so that's the way I'll be dealing with you. Don't be worrying about that other lot, be your own man and be done with it. You call me uncle. I know desert business, all right."

Alan stood warily, watching him, eyes glistening.

"Come on, mate, come and play some blues with me. Go get your stuff and bring it down to the music room, I'll wait for you here. We'll have a bit of a session, do you the world of good."

"Uncle? Which way?"

"Ah, Yatjimarra side. Father's mother side belong you. Further out."

"Is that right? That Andy, drunken bugger, you know. Can't hold his grog. Drove his old ute through the front window of the pub, did you know that? Bloody wasn't funny, made a real mess of the place. We had to put bollards in."

"Fair dinkum, eh? Yeah, that'd be right. How'd he get the grog?"

"Ah, that bloody rotten copper got him some, causing trouble, eh. That cop who got blown up, serves him right in a way. I don't like saying things like that, but he hurt my Dad too, more than once, and me, and Eddie. Not necessary, eh? He wanted to shoot my dog, just to be a shit."

By then Mr Carpenter was watching him closely.

"That's the way, Alan. Good lad. Now go get that horn of yours and we'll blow some music."

He waited there for him on the lawn until he got back, and leading the way across took some keys and opened the side door of a tall brick building. Inside was a fully equipped studio, with a stage and full theatre lighting, and sound-proofed walls and a bio-box high up on the other side.

While the teacher went around switching on a few lights Alan took his cornet and wiping it fit the mouth piece, and without thinking started limbering up with a soft melody, causing the other to stop and listen.

"What's that you're playing? I've heard it before, somewhere."

"Ah, well, you know, it's part of the opening theme from *The Butterfly Lover Concerto*, for oboe. Dr Zhang rearranged it for cornet for me, to help me with my breathing. Do you like it?"

There was another long pause. "It's lovely. You play so beautifully. This is phenomenal. I am sorry, I didn't realise. You were at Hilltop Primary, brass band. Mr Watson, the Salvation Army Captain. But you've been out in the desert all last year. Who taught you to play like that?"

"I already said, Dr Zhang. Gracie's father. Like, they all call him Sam Cheong, and he works as the hotel gardener, out at Ballard. He's a war veteran, and a doctor and a Confucian scholar, you know. He's also been teaching me classics, and philosophy. When I was at Walilya he taught me by radio; made sure I kept up with my practice and my reading, like, it's quiet there anyway and I could get away by myself and just play. Dr Jayaraman taught me as well. I think she might be a Buddhist nun or something, she didn't say. And Mr Baxter can play, and Mum."

The teacher was gazing steadily at him, brow furrowed.

"The past few days when we stopped off at Ballard, on the way here," Alan went on absently, thinking back, "Sam did some more practice with me, and helped me some more, like, advice mainly. He's very strict. I don't mean strict like in hard, I don't know, he's great, he just knows things. He taught me how to breathe properly, and gave me the right exercises to do."

"Alan, sorry to interrupt, you have an unusual *embouchure*. I'd like you to tell me about it."

"What? What's *embouchure*? What are you talking about?"

118

"Mouthing. The way you position your lips and cheeks. Do you blow up, or down?"

He had to stop and think for a moment. "No, just straight in. Cooling soup, you know, that's what Sam calls it. Dr Zhang, I mean. Blowing your soup cool, like, your cup of tea."

"Is that right? A boy your age. How very unusual. Do you mind if we have a few others come and join us?"

"Yeah, sure, all right. No worries."

Chapter Twenty Three

It was 8:30 before they finished music practice; more of a demonstration exercise. Alan packed his gear and turning to leave while the teachers sat discussing his technique said goodnight. He strolled easily across the broad expanse of lawn to the college building, and went straight up to his room and stripped for his evening shower. Taking his toilet bag and with a towel around his waist he wandered along the corridor trying to find the shower block.

Somebody poked his head out of an open doorway as he went past, pointing to the end of the building, and he nodded and smiled. The place was divided up into fairly open cubicles, and he went into one and hanging his towel on a hook opened the taps to stand there adjusting the water until the temperature was about right, and he stepped under.

He sensed movement behind him. There was a shadow in the doorway watching him.

"No nudity, Cameron," a voice said. "This is a decent school."

Whoever it was promptly pulled the plastic screen across and withdrew. As he showered he heard giggling and voices . . . hooligan . . . went to Hilltop . . . but when he dried himself and came out to comb his hair and brush his teeth, still not thinking he was naked, there was nobody there. He stood there puzzled for a long moment, and shrugged, then finishing wrapped the towel around himself and made his way back along the corridor to his room.

He hadn't been paying a lot of attention when he might have; his mind on his frustration and disappointment with the small wind ensemble Mr Carpenter called in to practice with him. That other music teacher with the sax, just blow the bloody thing, eh? Make the sound come out. And that senior student on the flute, supposed to be running for exhibition, play it for Christ's sake. It was all flat, dead, no life in it; no passion, no breathing or rhythm, no *chi*.

Aside from Chen Gang's *Butterfly Lovers*, Sam had played Artur Rubenstein for him on his old CD player, playing Greig's *Piano Concerto in A Minor*, and Tchaikovsky's *Piano Concerto in B♯ Minor*, and Bizet's *Carmen*, and de Falla's *Alicia de Larrocha*, and *Fantasía Bética*. And Malcolm McNab, Louis Armstrong, Wynton Marsalis, Chris Botti, Chuck Mangioni. And Frank Sinatra, really, Ella Fitzgerald, Erroll Garner, Lionel Hampton, Johnny Mathis, Nancy Wilson, Ray Stevens bit of fun; *Misty*. Gracie Cheong. Such loveliness his heart sang.

Setting that standard, helping him understand what excellence is; what to strive after.

His bed was way too soft, that was another thing, seriously. He tested the other bed, the same. He would have to get somebody to come and fix them, the janitor or whoever; put a board under the mattress or something.

In the meantime he pulled it off the bed and onto the floor. It was still too hot and his Mum wasn't there, so spreading a sheet on the mattress he lay down and went straight to sleep. During the night he sat up and pulling another sheet off the bed covered himself.

The ceiling light went on suddenly. Somebody tripped over him. Startled awake he looked up but the light blinded him and he buried his head back in the pillow. It was dark outside.

"Solly, so solly."

"What?"

"Solly. Solly. My name is Dexter. I Hong Kong. I your loom mate. I just allive Hong Kong. Two o'clock aeroplane."

"Ah, what? *Mh sí*. No worries."

"Oh, good, you speak Chinese. How you speak Chinese? Who teach you speak Chinese?"

"What? No, I can't. Only a little. *Siu siu*. Dr Zhang, that's all."

"Dr Zhang? You know Dr Zhang? Who is Dr Zhang?"

Alan buried his head back in his pillow, but then realising whatever it was wasn't going to go away stood suddenly and throwing the mattress back onto the bed spread the sheet over it, then the second sheet and a quilt from somewhere.

"Oh! You no clothes. Is allight. Sharing same loom. Two boys. Understand. No homosexual. Allight."

Alan gazed sleepily at the other boy for a long moment, bewildered, but then climbed into bed and went right back to sleep.

A siren rang, ripping his head apart. Dexter was there again, tapping him on the shoulder.

"Why you no wake up? Come, come. Time for waking up. Blekfass. Time for blekfass."

"What?"

"I Dexter. Your name Alan, OK? I your loom mate. Time for blekfass."

He turned over, rubbing his eyes. It was light outside, not too early, about 7:00. He rose and still not thinking stepped up out of the bed and started to dress. He went back along the corridor to the bathroom to wash and comb his hair, other boys standing aside to make way for him. Both in their new school uniform the two emerged into the corridor and joined the queue down toward the dining room.

Somebody was sniggering.

For the first time he turned to look at Dexter. He was all right, just a kid like himself, nothing out of the ordinary. Just arrived in town, confused and wondering, nervous, wanting a friend.

The voices kept on. He glanced about. Nothing.

"Hooligan . . . Hilltop . . . no upbringing . . . bloody psycho . . . no sense of humour . . ."

After a long pregnant pause Alan stepped out of line and said in a loud voice, "Anyone with anything to say to me can say it to my face, all right."

The place went silent, but then a piping voice came at him, "Whoa, Nitro, off you go. Boom!"

He spun around. The other made the mistake of ducking suddenly behind a bigger boy who moved slightly to cover him, but by then it was too late. He simply lost it.

In three steps he shoved the bigger boy aside and grabbed the other by the throat, slamming him against the wall.

"Take it back!" he was yelling, face red by now and eyes narrowed in anger, tears streaming down his cheeks.

"Take it back, I said," but the other boy had his breath stopped and couldn't say anything.

Alan felt strong hands holding him, pulling him away.

"Not like that. No good like that. Let 'im go, all right."

"Allan, stop, you choking 'im, that boy. Let 'im go."

The familiar accents distracted him momentarily and he relaxed his grip. He turned to see a pair of dark faces next to his and knew the smell of them. He pushed the other boy away, who tripped and went sprawling.

By then some of the teachers were there. All the other boys backed off to form a wide circle around him, frightened now, staring at him. The two older desert boys were still holding him by the arms, and with a worried glance at the teachers led him away from the scene, outside to the lawn where they sat on the grass not saying anything to one another.

Twenty minutes later one of the teachers poked his head out the door, calling across for him to come inside and the other two go and have their breakfast.

The teacher led him all the way through the great labyrinth of a building to emerge near the front facing the main road, across the foyer into the principal's office. He could hear the traffic outside. Mr Carpenter was there, and the principal, and some other people.

"Hey, Alan, how are you, mate?"

"Yeah, I'm all right. What?"

"Ah, don't you want to know how Simon is? He's in the infirmary, lying down."

He looked blankly at him a moment, then shrugged, shaking his head. "Who's Simon?"

"The boy you tried to throttle."

"What? No, I didn't. What are you talking about? He needs to apologise to me. I'll go and see him. I want to hear him apologise. And a few of the others."

"Ah, Alan, sorry," one of the others said, "but you tried to kill him. His throat is badly bruised and he's unable to speak. When you pushed him he hit his head, probable concussion. You don't know your own strength, perhaps. For your sake we won't be pressing charges, but we do need to get to the bottom of this."

He sat there for a long moment, brows furrowed. "How would I know?" he asked finally. "I just got here, only yesterday afternoon. I don't know anybody, hell, they don't know me either. I haven't had a chance. They are saying all those things about me, that I don't even know myself. I need somebody to tell me what's going on."

The principal was watching him, and leaned forward slightly. "That boy you hurt. If it was up to us we can accept your explanation. We might have taken more care perhaps, but what's done is done. The simple fact of the matter is that his father happens to be the state attorney-general. It will be in the papers. Are you following me?"

"What? No, not really. What's that, some sort of government minister or something?"

"Well, yes. He is the senior law officer in this jurisdiction, and a member of cabinet."

"Is that right?" Alan was thinking, but not the way they thought.

"That's what's wrong here, isn't it?" he said finally. "What we need is a change of government, if it's those sorts of people running the place."

Chapter Twenty Four

"I don't bloody care, Mum. That's not what I'm saying. Everybody knows everything about me except me, and I'm tired of it."

They'd been arguing for miles. Very good thing she was still in town and hadn't left yet. What would he have done then? I would have got a taxi. But all your money is locked up, how could you afford it? Well, you'd have to pay the fare then, wouldn't you?

Whatever she said, he was going back to Ballard and that was it.

She hadn't asked him whether he wanted to move to Ballard in the first place, but that wasn't the question either. And no it's not Gracie, I'm not that horny, or disrespectful. And no it's not Dad, well yes it is in a way because I miss him a lot and he's buried there. I don't want to talk about Dad.

"What do you want to talk about, Alan?"

"Nothing, all right?"

About 50 kilometres later he turned to her and said, "Mum, is it possible do you think to have an intelligent conversation, I mean, with grownups? Not with old people, I don't mean that, but you grownups?"

Further along the road, without glancing at him, she said simply, "Say what you need to say, Alan."

"Well, what I want to say is, when you were a girl you grew up on a famous cattle station with all your famous brothers, isn't it. I don't know anything about Dad, only he was in some war, and Yatjimarra said his family lived in Sydney, or somewhere."

"What about that, Alan?"

"Well I grew up in a pub, and I went to Hilltop Primary School, then we went to Ballard, and I lost my Dad. What I do know about, seriously, is living in a pub. I know about pubs. That's my life. I know about the bar, and the house, and the bottleshop and the banking, and doing the till. I know how to set the table properly, and chopping vegetables and peeling spuds. It's what I know. That's why I'm going to live in Ballard. It's what I understand. I'm very good at it. I don't have to put up with bullshit from jumped-up idiots."

A little further on she said to him, "You neglected to mention fine musician, son."

"Yes, that too. Those teachers at Bridgefield are hopeless. Same mistakes I used to make."

"So why didn't you tell me about your plans for Ballard? I saw it on the TV. That's the first I knew of it. Mum, you should have said something to me first. That's not fair."

"Well, at least now I know what *embouchure* is," he went on, when she didn't answer, almost to himself. "That's one thing at least."

This time she did glance his way.

"Alan, yes, maybe I should have spent more time with you. I apologise. We have simply been so busy, that's all. Is there anything else?"

"Yes. Why didn't you tell me about Uncle Ken?"

"Ken? My brother Ken? What about him? He has nothing to do with anything."

"Yes he does."

"In what way?"

"He's the one who shot that Barry fella. You know, the big bikie, at Dad's funeral."

"What? What are you saying? He wasn't even there."

"Yes he was. We saw his tracks. Yatjimarra. He wouldn't make a mistake like that. He was certain. It was him all right."

"Why would he do that?"

"How would I bloody know, Mum? That's what I mean, isn't it?"

Chapter Twenty Five

Eddie had already moved back into their old bedroom, somehow knowing Alan would be back. They didn't say anything much to one another, except the following day when Eric arrived foot-sore and badly undernourished from Walilya and Eddie smiled knowingly.

The mood about the place was different. Monique in the kitchen was bossing everyone about mercilessly, and Veronica was back making the breakfasts. When she put food out for Eric he wolfed it down, then lay down on a chaff bag and slept for two days. He wasn't a pup anymore but had grown to full size; not a big dog and his balls seemed enormous.

Eddie too was pubic, like him, with soft down on his upper lip and a crack in his voice. He hadn't paid much attention when he was here last week, his mind on Gracie, but now they were in the same room again it was hard to miss. He didn't mind. They both loved the freedom. One day he would find out who that girl was he was promised to; he'd make a point of it. Returning the tacit compliment, watching him he reminded himself that Eddie would make a fine husband, and a good father, and Eddie sensing the thought in him warmed to him once more.

Life back the way they it be. Almost.

Sam refused to allow them to rest on their laurels. They were growing boys. Now that he had them back with him, bringing Gracie with him every morning he was up early to take them all through their *tài jí quán* exercises, especially focused on breathing and *qigong* awareness and body movement, teaching them the soft *neijia* techniques - the internal arts - getting their bodies properly primed for the day ahead. He made special boy soup for them, and cooked them meals, for their body he explained when he brought them over; you glowing boy, must be healthy; good bone, muscle, brain, strong body, clear skin, so important OK.

Sam saw his father in him, pain behind soft green-brown eyes; life pain of inherently kind and gentle men witness to violence, which unable to comprehend it or come to terms with it without wise counsel made them dangerous. He knew of Alan's loss of temper, and while he said nothing nonetheless kept a close eye on him, through discipline and exercise steering him away from his pain while keeping thought from his mind that some time he might use his martial arts and seriously hurt somebody.

After the *tài jí quán* they were allowed to have their breakfast.

The rest of the day quickly settled into their old routine. It was plain that nobody was going to allow him to dwell on things. Dan was managing the bar now but not doing too good a job of the bottleshop, so Alan took over from him, then did the till and the banking. Mrs Robinson smiled when she saw him back, but didn't say anything either.

That done they had to do their school work, which didn't take long. At a school most of the day was taken up in regimentation, and in high school moving about from class to class, but here at home they could get through their homework in three good hours as Monique practiced her bossing on them, before she went across to start on the kitchen. After a late lunch Gracie went across to the hotel for her singing and elocution lessons while Sam came over to the house again to teach music. It was plain that he and Mum had been in deep discussion about the two of them, swapping notes to ensure their program was consistent.

He was interested in what the teacher had been saying to Alan about *embouchure*, and gave him additional mouthing and tonguing exercises he could do while going about his chores. Most of all he did not want him pushing too hard, forcing the life-breath as he called it, considering it inauspicious and harmful to his developing body. They would play together occasionally, but as often they just sat and talked quietly, or read from some of the texts he'd given him, when Bunna would appear as usual from out of nowhere. What Sam wanted Alan to do was explore the music within himself, and play from that not from his lessons, or from sheet music, so what he did was start carrying a spare mouthpiece around in his pocket and used that to exercise with.

Eddie wanted more of his time; tired of sitting with Dan and Harry ignoring him pretty much, so after music they usually saddled the horses brought back down from Walilya for them and went riding, but after that he had to start in the kitchen with Monique who he decided was going to teach him to be a chef. Mum was being less remote, but at the same time she worked with him more closely now as a junior employee; a cadet, and he acknowledged the new courtesy toward him though she made sure he knocked off by 8:30 or 9:00 at the latest and went to bed on time and got plenty of sleep.

When the hotel was busy with busloads of tourists the pace was hectic, but they made up the difference between buses when he and Eddie rode further out, or he sat playing or simply doing his *embouchure* exercises with the mouth piece, and reading Gracie's letters to him that she left in the hotel's internal mailbox, and writing back.

One day she wrote informing him that she was no longer to be known as Gracie Cheong, but as Miss Grace Zhang, so that night he sat out on the back porch after he knocked off and played his cornet to her for well over an hour, until Bunna or somebody called out from somewhere telling him to can it, or he'd stick the bloody thing up you know where.

Days ran into weeks. Eric followed him everywhere, not always at heel but keeping him in sight. If he was in the house the dog was on the front porch, and when he was in the hotel he was on the back veranda. When they went riding he loped along after them. One Sunday morning he and Eddie rode across to the graveyard where he'd left a small banister brush so he could sweep the dust and leaves off his Dad's grave, and do Barry's while he was at it. Nobody came to visit Bad Barry, the Good Bloke, and he thought that was sad. The bikie gang was long gone and he wondered at times about them; where they might be now. Walking back across between the old gravestones something made him remember, to stop and think, and stepping into line with his father's grave stood where he'd been playing that morning.

He glanced over at Eddie, then stepping around the grave started pacing in direct line with it, counting as he went, trying to keep his paces about a metre apart. Past a good 870 metres or so he ran into a small rocky stream bed that ran along under the looming escarpment and drained he guessed into the waterhole where they swam, when it did rain sometime. He stepped down into it, and casting about saw a spent cartridge case over to his left, coloured and dull now from eight months of exposure to the elements, and he went over and picked it up.

Coming back up he showed it to Eddie, who stared at it for a long moment before looking him in the eye.

"What you want to do with that?" was all he said. "Throw it away. No good that business."

But Alan kept looking at it, turning it over and over. Most of it was still brassy, though dull now. It had a thick dark stripe up one side where it had lain on the ground, with a greenish spot next to it from an old bird dropping or something it had been touching. He put it in his pocket, and turned to mount his horse when Eric pricked his ears up and stood sharply alert, watching the main road.

A dirty old white minibus came along, battered and covered with red dust, somebody calling out to them.

When they rode back to the house the small bus was parked there behind the hotel. They saw Reuben there, or Eric did first and bounded happily over to greet him, tail furiously wagging.

Alan dismounted as people got out of the bus. Aside from Reuben was his brother Danny; his cousin-brother properly who he knew from the dormitory, and three girls. Last of all Andy and Alice stepped out, and then Teddy Scott who'd been driving. Grace came out of the hotel, she must have been with Mum, and seeing her there crossed to one of the girls to hug her, smiling.

He turned around to Eddie who had also dismounted by then but was standing behind his horse, hiding. When he looked at him he was grinning from ear to ear, giggling almost, tears running down his cheeks, plainly embarrassed. If he was a white boy he'd be red as a beetroot. His moleskins were tenting and he spun about to stand with his back to him.

He glanced back at the two girls. Grace had the other by the arm, leaning forward with her other hand cupping her mouth, whispering something in her ear. The other girl glanced in his direction and smiled. She wasn't pretty as pretty girls go but remarkably handsome, with a nice smile and laughing eyes.

He ducked behind the horse again and said to Eddie. "Ha! That's her isn't it? Wife belong you, eh? Right, no more gammon me, eh? Owe you nothing. You'll be right. Now we're even."

With a big grin he turned again and taking the reins from him pulled his horse away leaving Eddie exposed in the open, and seeing him there everyone smiled. Eddie turned his head shyly to catch her eye, but then promptly walked across to the house and disappeared inside.

Alan looked after him for a long moment, and then leading the horses across asked her.

"What's your name? I'm Alan. Brother belong you, eh? Husband belong Miss Gracie Zhang, that one, properly."

She didn't answer, until Grace said quietly, "This one Valerie, Alan. Name, Valery Scott. That Reuben cousin-sister, Danny sister,

133

properly, that boy there. Same mother, same father. Call 'im that Teddy Scott uncle, father side. You right, wife belong that Eddie, brother belong me."

Then she turned to the other two girls.

"This one girl Frances Yatjimarra; sister belong Reuben, different father. This one, Evie Scott, same mother, same father Reuben."

He gazed at Frances, looking too much like that Andy for comfort. By then Alice had come over to him and was holding him, gently stroking his arms and back and crying over him, while Yatjimarra himself stood close beside her rubbing his armpit sweat on him.

"That Alice frighten for you, Alan" Gracie went on, her voice soft. "Worry for you, all this time, crying for you. That old man worry for you too much, go away city, maybe can't come back. Everybody missing you. Singing you, come back this place. Belong this place now."

"'Nuff that worry bijnitch," Teddy was saying, grumpy and anxious to get away before it got late. "Orright now, everybody 'appy. All you mob, kid mob, give me 'and with suitcase, bags, everyt'ing, orright."

Alan turned to shake Reuben's hand, then Danny's. A quick glance across at Teddy told him they were to be sleeping in the house, in the spare room next to him and Eddie. The three girls were to being living in Sam's big old house with Veronica and Alice, while Andy that Yatjimarra randy drunken bastard would be living in the single men's demountable with Bunna; Dan and Harry keeping pretty much to themselves still in the old sleepout.

"No bloody grog that fella, orright. Better make sure. You boss for that Andy grog bijnitch, Alan. No more bullshit."

But he wasn't paying that much attention, instead watching Gracie now with friends to keep her company, and he couldn't stop smiling in her direction. She kept smiling back, but then she disappeared behind Valerie and wouldn't let him look at her. Valerie glanced sternly over at him, brows furrowed, and taking the hint he turned his attention to Danny and Reuben.

The thought came suddenly into his head they would have to take turns at the swimming hole now, girls and boys separate, and he blushed at the thought of it. The two boys were staring at him too, grinning, and he realised his pants were tenting as well so he picked up one of the bags and carried it over to the house in front of him.

"Yeah, shut up, all right," he muttered on the way past. "Just jealous, isn't it."

Teddy had turned the bus around and was already heading out to the roadhouse to refuel for the trip back to Walilya. They didn't have time after that for much settling in because Mum was there telling them all lunch would be in the dining room in 15 minutes and they were to be clean and tidy.

Chapter Twenty Six

The four girls were far better organised, showering quickly and changing into clean white blouses and skirts, and did their hair while the boys talking non-stop had simply combed their hair and came as they were. It didn't go unnoticed. Mum carried on anyway.

What she had to say first, once they finished their meal, is that the company had also finally purchased the roadhouse; put on the market through high fuel prices and declining sales, with travellers topping up their fuel tanks along the highway. They were entering a new arrangement with the fuel company on a discount scheme for their hotel clients, and stimulus packages for the bus companies.

She spoke slowly and deliberately. They had tried to get Tim Grant down here in his role in community policing, now senior constable, but he had opted for Lake Marnma with its bigger school and better football team and they would have to wait a little to find the right person. In the meantime they would have to put up with whoever was sent.

The reason the others were here from Walilya is for training in catering and hospitality; it was something of an experiment in creating local employment but it was important that the project be made to work. That was the reason you especially were selected. They still did not have enough children for a school to be established so they would continue with their home-schooling, though when she said that she was looking pointedly in Alan's direction.

He might have been paying closer attention, but at that moment he was fingering the cartridge case in his pocket. The others being here now would work out OK as far as he was concerned, he was thinking; at least Gracie wouldn't be so lonely, and whoever it was he could help to learn the bottleshop, and the till and the banking.

What he missed was that he would be working over at the roadhouse, not the hotel, or heard but didn't believe it.

When Mum finished she dismissed the girls but told the boys to remain seated. She was not at all happy with them, and came over and told them so.

"Now, you boys," she said. "I specifically asked you to be here in clean clothes, and with your hair done. At the hotel here, to make it work we must set the standard. If you're unable to follow a simple instruction like that, I'm afraid have something else for you to do."

"What? Really?"

"I don't have enough staff at the roadhouse yet. Ray and Peg are staying on; it's hard enough to get good people way out here without losing them for no reason, but we are going to be open from 7:00 am to 11:00 pm, in three shifts. I'd do the rosters, and let you know."

"Ah, come on Mum. I've got my job here."

She gazed down at him, and sighed. "Alan, learn to listen finally. You pay no attention to the rest of the staff, and it's becoming uncomfortable. You have to do much better than that."

He stared up at her, and was about to argue with her when Eddie piped up.

"That right, Alan. Can't listen properly, you fella. No good. Been telling you can't listen, eh? Need to wake up."

Alan turned to stare at him now, but the other two boys were watching him as well, plainly in agreement with Eddie but too shy yet to say anything to him; uncomfortable with it.

He gazed off into the distance for a long moment, eyes glistening, then back to his mother.

"What about the bottleshop."

"Yes, that's all right," she replied, gently. "That is your thing, and you do a good job of it. You can do the shop at the roadhouse too if you like. I like your displays, and the way you highlight certain lines we need to move, very creative. Our sales are good. All right then, you know what you have to do."

"What about the till and the bank?"

She turned to Eddie, cutting Alan off from further discussion; saying quietly to herself, almost as an aside, "I'm sure Grace can add and subtract."

"Ed, what time do you and Bunna finish your cutting-up, and getting the meat in the fridge?"

"Ah, 8:00 o'clock, missus. That fella finish 7:00 o'clock, no worry. I do packing, cleaning up, 8:00 o'clock all right, same every morning."

"She's not missus, Ed."

"Sorry. Missus Cameron."

Elsie glanced from one to the other, hiding her smile. Two bright boys attuned to each other, neither of them prepared to give way.

"Can you start earlier, get up with Alan, and have your breakfast and be finished by seven?"

Eddie thought for a moment, then looked up and nodded.

She turned to Reuben and Danny. They both shrugged, so she turned to leave.

"All of you, you boys," she said on the way out, "when I ask you to do something that's what I want you to do. Do you understand?"

"Mum, is that copper's mate still there? Who are Ray and Peg, anyway?"

"No, son, he's gone. The condition of sale was that he not open another business locally, or set himself up in competition with us. Sorry, but I don't know where he is. Ray and Peg Smith have been there since June, brought in as managers after that accident on the road; while you were at Walilya."

She left, and the four boys glanced at one another. Eddie stood first.

"Go and have a look, eh?"

The place was about 1200 metres along the highway from the turnoff, about three quarters of a mile in the old measure, and it took the four boys only around 20 minutes walking.

Bunna was there at one of the bowsers pumping petrol while people stood around stretching their legs, and gave them only a quick nod as they went past and entered the building.

Inside was clean but the smell was rank. Some old Country and Western music was playing through cracked speakers. Slim Whitman. Yeah, Slim Whitman, eh? But, sounds like shit.

They all lined up at the lunch bar, appearing as if they wanted to buy Chiko Rolls, or pies, and the lady came up to them smiling. Then she recognised them and smiled again.

"Ah, just looking around," Alan said to her, smiling back. "Mum said we have to come up and give you a hand sometimes."

He shrugged, looking around, still smiling, and started to turn to introduce his friends. But by then people from the cars outside were coming in wanting hamburgers, so he stepped aside to let them be served. He stood back a moment more looking around, but then suddenly with one hand down next to his leg he signalled to the other boys and they all turned and trooped out.

Chapter Twenty Seven

"Come and talk to me, Alan. I'm not putting up with this. Enough!"

There was a long silence.

"That your Mummy talking you, Alan, properly, titty mother," Eddie was saying, breaking the quiet. "Love you so much. Can't say no."

He was lying on his side, facing the wall. Walking back from that shit of a roadhouse past the graveyard, and the new, fairly new, earthworks and bitumen and blue metal there in the middle of the road, right across the road, at that spot anyway, he stopped and went off into the bush by himself leaving the others standing there staring after him.

There was old wallpaper in front of his face and he ran his fingers up and down it, absorbing his gaze while he listened with his ears, and his thoughts.

He rolled onto his back, looking across to the other bed.

"You telling me I can't listen, can't see, that right? All the time, Eddie. Everybody. Think I'm stupid. Depends on what you're looking at, unna?"

But when he glanced over his way he could see Eddie had been crying, worrying about him. Too much. Not just jiggy-jig bijnitch with sister; brother-in-law looking after sister, looking after kid mob. Crying for him. Properly.

He knew Mum was still there, outside, frustrated with him. He could hear it in her voice.

"All right," he called to her finally. "Fifteen minutes, OK? We'll be right. Sorry about before. Fifteen minutes. We'll be there. Your office. Mum."

But he still didn't go. As he rose Sam came in. They could hear him speaking to Mum and she left, then knocking quietly on the door. Eddie let his father in, then sat back on his bed without saying anything. He flicked his gazed back at Alan.

Sam stood there a moment, observing him, then sat next to him on the bed. He had been half up but Sam placed his hand on his shoulder and had him lie down again.

"You not well, Alan." He said softly. "You want talk to me about it?"

"I'm all right, Sam. What are you worrying about?"

"No, you are not well. You want talk to me about it?"

"No, I'm all right, I said. What do you want me to talk to you about?"

"No, is OK. No worry. Is not your fault. Nobody blaming you."

"What? Blaming me for what? What are you talking about?"

"Accident. Not your fault, OK? Stop blaming yourself. Is finished, long time now. Time for you stop it now, settle down, no more worry that business, allight?"

"I'm not worrying. It's not me. Why are you blaming me? I trust you, Sam, you're my teacher. Why are you talking to me like that?"

"Because, what happen outside, just now. Before. What going on?"

"What? Nothing happened. Nothing's going on. Stop talking to me like that."

Sam turned to Eddie, who simply shrugged.

"You blackout, Alan. Collapse. What's going on? Let me help you."

"Nothing. Why do I need you to help me? Nothing happened. We were coming back from the roadhouse, that's all."

"So, what you doing in bed? How you get into bed? What going on with you? Is allight, you tell me."

Alan looked up, staring at him, then down at his bed, and his body lying on it, and blinked.

Sam reached over and with the ball of his thumb gently began rubbing his forehead, between his eyebrows, and he closed his eyes.

When he looked up again Jim was there in his wheelchair, and Paddie. He smiled at them and was about to say something to them when he noticed Dan and Harry standing there as well, and Uncle Ken and Uncle Greg. Frank was there too, and Andy and Bunna, but he couldn't see how they could all fit into the bedroom.

He was thinking about it; how come the room was big now, and where was the wallpaper and the pattern that was just there a minute ago, but Old Jim was saying something to him.

"You talk to Dr Zhang, young fella. Cut the crap. No more bullshit, orright."

He looked across at him and tried to say something, but then he noticed he was crying. When he tried to say something he just kept crying. Paddie was sitting there next to Eddie on his bed, holding his hand, and Poppie Jim in his wheelchair. Sam was still sitting next to him on the bed, watching over him as he lay there. He got that part right. He was sure of it. His four uncles were lounging against the walls, and in the doorway. Harry was rolling himself a cigarette.

But he couldn't stop crying. They all waited and waited for him, nobody making a move to stop him, or pass a handkerchief, or anything you normally expect, if you were crying, or sad about something. Nobody moved to do anything.

It took what seemed like eons before something or other made him think why was he crying? I didn't do anything. Why am I crying?

He shook his head and reached into his pocket for the spent cartridge. Then he sat up with it, and handed it across to Ken.

"Well, what I was going to ask you, Uncle Ken, but I forgot, is what sort of round is that?"

The other took it, and turned it around between his fingers. He looked at the end, next to the primer, then leaned forward to show him.

"See there, son? That stamping on there? It's a .243 marksman round."

"Really? Do you mean, like sniper's use?"

"No, it's not a military calibre. I don't even know that roo shooters use them much; generally they'll use a .222 or .223. I know a couple of the fellas who use a .17, mostly foxes, eh?"

"Know anyone with a rifle like that, that fires them?"

"Yes, I do. Want me to show you sometime?"

"Ah, later. Not now. Wait until Christmas, all right. You can show me then. Will that be all right, show me then, Christmas I mean?"

"Sure. Take a few shots, if you like, see how good you are."

He glanced up at him.

"You're a good shot, eh? Uncle Ken. Andy reckons, anyway. He said you're a state champion, but maybe he was bullshitting to me."

"No, it's not bullshit. Show you my trophies too if you like."

"So you can shoot."

"Yes, sure. Why do you ask?"

"Because I want to know why you shot Barry."

They all stood still, watching him.

"Because it was a job that had to be done, Alan. Just a job."

"No, that's not right. It's not just a job, it can't be. It was Dad's funeral, and you ruined it."

Ken hung his head at that, and said softly, "For that I'm sorry, Alan. I couldn't see. It was a chance I took, only because the shot was right and I had to get it off. I apologise, do you believe me? I couldn't see what was happening, and that copper was right up my arse. That's it."

"No, that's not it . . ."

But somehow the thought passed and he couldn't think what to say next. Ken didn't seem to be there anymore.

". . . vaulting arrogance . . ." Uncle Greg was saying to somebody. "Unbelievable assumption of entitlement . . . crippling incompetence . . . fucking unbelievable . . ."

"That's about it," . . . somebody else . . . "Greg works right there on The Terrace . . . slap bang in the thick of it . . . knows how to put things into words . . ."

His Dad was looking down at him, smiling.

He was little and in his pyjamas, just out of the bath with his teeth clean and hair combed and Daddy was tucking him in.

Chapter Twenty Eight

"Sorry, Mum."

"That's all right, Alan. We're all under pressure. Feeling better?"

"Yep. I'm OK. What do you want to see me about?"

"Well, the roadhouse, isn't it?" she replied. "What do you want to do with it?"

"Me? What would I do with it? I'd gut the place, tear everything out. It's terrible. No wonder they're going broke."

"What would you do first?"

"That food bar. It's rancid. No reason to be buying in all that takeaway stuff and frying it, or us trying to run two kitchens. It's silly. We can supply them with food from here, that's nice and fresh. We can do cold-cuts, and salads and sandwiches. If they want hamburgers we can do them fresh."

Mum was jotting down notes as he spoke and he leaned over her shoulder following her.

"All right, next, install a really nice sound system, 7 speakers, you know, digital. Brighten the place up. But we still need to do the floor coverings, and repaint the whole place, so we might as well throw that old stock out and install new shelving."

He stopped for a while, thinking, and she turned to watch his face.

"Mum, another thing, you know, it's too American, like something in some dumb movie. Why don't we feature local custom instead? What's so hot about old Country and Western? Why don't we have *Tjuma Pulka* Aboriginal Radio through the new sound system? We can be selling Uncle Harry's belts, and whips and bridles, saddles even. I bet a lot of people would come down here to buy things than go all the way across to Kal."

"Anything else?"

"Mining stuff. We can have tools, and spare parts. The motor car stuff they have is all right, but it's hell old stock, Mum. It's covered in dust. Their display is no good, and it's all down the back. They'll never sell anything like that. I bet people driving through have something wrong with their car. Must be. There's nothing else between here and the border. The REPCO traveller or Auto One, somebody like that, must come through, like they do for our bottleshop, so he can keep an eye on it. We should get in good new stock, and get rid of that old stuff."

She finished her notes, and taking out the loose sheets reached across for a big thick manila folder on the shelf above her desk.

Alan sat, and busying herself with the filing she turned her head to look at him.

"But there's something else, Mum, isn't there?"

"What might that be, son?"

"I won't be doing it, will I?"

"No, you won't."

"I'm going back to that school, aren't I?"

"Yes. You're learning. In case you wish to argue, it was not my decision."

He looked away, past her. "Poppie Jim made, like, an executive decision, didn't he. Tell me, I want to know."

"Alan, you know what you need to know. That's it. What I can tell you is that we are setting extra money aside to send Eddie with you, and Reuben and Danny if you really want to know. We have two more houses now in Applecross and Maylands, in your name. They will help pay for it, and there's some grant money available should we need it."

He paused, still thinking, still wanting to argue.

"Mum, I don't want to study music, is that all right? I want to do something else."

"Dear boy," she said with a long sigh. "Decide what you want to do, will you do that for me? I recommend you simply focus on the core disciplines, don't worry about the rest. Get your Maths and Physics and Chemistry out of the way, and English, and some elective like Biology or Earth Sciences or something. Just concentrate on them. We want you at university, is that clear?"

She reached over and took his hand, saying gently, "We only need to know that you're ready for it, can cope with being away. Let me know how you are feeling, all right. If there's anything we can help you with, Alan, don't be bottling it up. Give me a ring will you, any time you're not feeling too good, or feel a bit lost. Call Sam if you like, though I doubt he's much good over the phone. Promise me that at least."

He had no chance to answer. By then Eddie was standing in the doorway looking for him, the news written all over his face.

Chapter Twenty Nine

Pop drove down from Lake Marnma to take them up to the interstate railway line and catch the train. Nobody was driving all the way to Perth and back again just to drop them off. He brought a couple of new boys with him from his school, replacing the four who were leaving now, along with three men and another lady to help Bunna and Andy, and pump fuel at the roadhouse.

They could always run the hotel short staffed, taking up the slack between bus runs when they were quiet with no house guests and miners in the bar; sometimes during the day but generally crowded later, but with the roadhouse to operate too now they'd all have their hours cut out for them.

The boys were packed and ready to go when they arrived, but Alan couldn't find the cartridge case anywhere. Finally he asked Eddie what Ken had done with it.

"What, Ken? Nothing."

"No, I mean, what did Ken do with it after I gave it to him the other day."

"No Ken, not here. Home Lake. You dreaming. What you talking about?"

He turned to Sam to ask him, but he said the same thing, that he'd been asleep.

"No, I wasn't. Ken was there, with Greg, and Poppie Jim and old Paddie. Yes, he was there, everyone was there. You and Eddie were there too. I'm sure of it. You must have seen them."

"Nothing, Alan," Eddie insisted. "You sleeping. Look in your pocket, eh? You keep it in your pocket."

He glanced anxiously from one to the other, then checked his pockets, but these were clean trousers. He thought for a moment before running over to the laundry to catch Andy.

"Andy, my dirty pants, did you clean out the pockets?"

"Eh? Nothing. All 'im pocket stuff there, look. That box there, orright?"

He went across to the window. There was an old tin box on the ledge full of odds and ends; bric-a-brac, small pieces of rock, bits of wire and string, old coins, cigarette lighters and a rusty pocket knife. There were a few old .22 bullets intact, and a .22 Hornet with a couple more .303 rounds, but no spent cartridge case of any sort.

Pop was calling to him to hurry up, they were leaving, and as he hesitated he heard the engine start and somebody blowing the horn.

Andy was saying to him, "Go on. Get goin'. I look around, orright."

He ran outside again. Eddie was sitting in the back with Danny in the middle and Reuben at the other window, and made him sit in the front with Pop.

Slamming the door shut he made to turn around again wanting to know what Eddie was on about. He wasn't sleeping he knew he was awake talking to Uncle Ken, but then he remembered suddenly Dad was there too. He stopped and went pale, broke out in a cold sweat, goose bumps tingling up and down his body, then he hung his head and after a long moment instead looked up to gaze out the car window.

The great long interstate train would be stopping to pick them up around 9:30 that night, at the freight siding just out of Lake Marnma, to arrive at City East interstate platform sometime after 7:30 tomorrow morning.

There was no hurry to get there, they had all afternoon and would have dinner with Nanna and Pop at their house before boarding the train. Sometimes it took over half an hour or more to load and unload, not a lot because the freight service came through earlier in the day loaded with sea containers, but paperwork and holdups because interstate mail and deliveries mainly.

Even then the drive took 3½ hours. They had to stop to pee twice, and stretch their legs, and Alan took the chance to get Danny sitting in the front while he sat in the back between Reuben and Eddie. They'd been talking about footie, and began pressing him for information about the new school, and what sort of players they had on their team, but he didn't know. All he said was if they play football as well as they play music they'd piss on them, seriously, from a very great height, making Danny turn around and laugh; face lighting up in sheer delight at the prospect.

That broke the ice.

By the time they were finally aboard the train they were tired, and full from Nanna's cooking. They laid their cases down between the seats, tilting the forward seats back to make a more or less bumpy level bed for themselves, and then heads and feet about with two single blankets they slept pretty much all the way through.

There was a car waiting for them at City East. Mr Carpenter. They shook hands all round and piled in.

Chapter Thirty

"*Hóu*! Alan! Is that you? You come back. Good. Much better now. Oh, so happy! *Néih hóu ma?*"

They turned to see who it was calling after them. It was Dexter.

"*Hóu, m̀h'gōi*. Dexter."

"Ah, you have some fliend. Better for you now, no so lonely. No good lonely."

Alan introduced Dexter to his friends. He was astonished when Eddie came out and said to him, "*Hóu*, Dexter. *Hahng'wúih*."

"Oh, also you speak Cantonese. Yes, very nice to meet you also. *Chíngmahn dím chīngfū?*"

"Ah, Eddie. Eddie Cheong. Properly, *Zhang Wu-cai*."

"Oh, such a good name. Velly good name for boy. So, your father Dr Zhang. I know about Dr Zhang. Alan tell about Dr Zhang, his teacher. So good, now you are here. But you are mix. Who is your mother, what country she flom?"

"This one country. Not this place, 'nother mob. Lake Marnma people."

Mr Carpenter interrupted at that point, telling Dexter he could catch up with them later. Right now they had a meeting with the principal.

As they made their way down the long corridor Alan nudged Eddie.

"You didn't tell me you had a proper Chinese name, and could speak Cantonese."

"Didn't ask me, unna."

"So what other languages can you speak that I don't know about?"

"*Wangai, Wuwala, Ngaanyatjarra, Antakarinya,* boss. And Mandarin."

"What about Grace? Can she speak them too?"

"Course, what you think? She speak *Yankunytjatjara, Kulpantja,* everything. Properly clever."

"But your English is terrible, both of you. Blackfella English, rubbish. Why don't you speak properly?"

"You Cantonese terrible, unna, can't speak *Wangai*, nothing. That English language rubbitch, can't say nothing properly. *Katepa,* stupid whitefella, you mob. Know nothing."

Danny walking right behind them began to giggle at the exchange. Reuben clipped him on the back of the head and he shut up, then the teacher turned with his finger to his lips telling them to be quiet.

Observing the familiar smiling banter and casual intimacy among the boys he gazed over at Alan.

"Feeling better now, Mr Cameron, are we? Bit more confidence, is that right?"

"Yes, sir."

"Not going to be putting up with any more bullshit now, are we?"

"No, sir. Except, sir . . ."

"Yes?"

"I'm not enrolling in music, all right. I'm just doing the straight academic subjects. I don't care what anybody thinks. And we're playing footie, right? The four of us."

"Any particular reason?"

"Well, yes, there is. But you mightn't like it."

"Try me."

"Yes, sir. It's because they're a bunch of pansies, can't play music for shit. And I'm only going to be frustrated with it."

"Fair enough. Brave answer. Do me a favour, all right, and don't tell them that. Just do your school work, and play your footie. Do your own time here, and let them do theirs."

"Yes, sir."

"And I want you in the swimming squad, that's the deal. Four o'clock every morning, until Easter. If you're going to be blowing that horn the way I think you should, you'll need to develop your chest and lungs. Dr Zhang tells me your *embouchure* is coming along nicely. We'll build on that, OK?"

"Did he? Well, yes sir. Thank you, sir."

THE END

ABOUT THE AUTHOR

As an anthropologist, novelist and writer Gil Hardwick is a gifted and imaginative author. Over many years working as a field ethnographer in the vast Australian inland he has met real characters and had real-life adventures, bringing his personalities and his plots to vibrant life. Writing from life, he neither shies away from real social issues and at times confronting dilemmas.

Well worth reading.